ELECTRONIC BRAIN

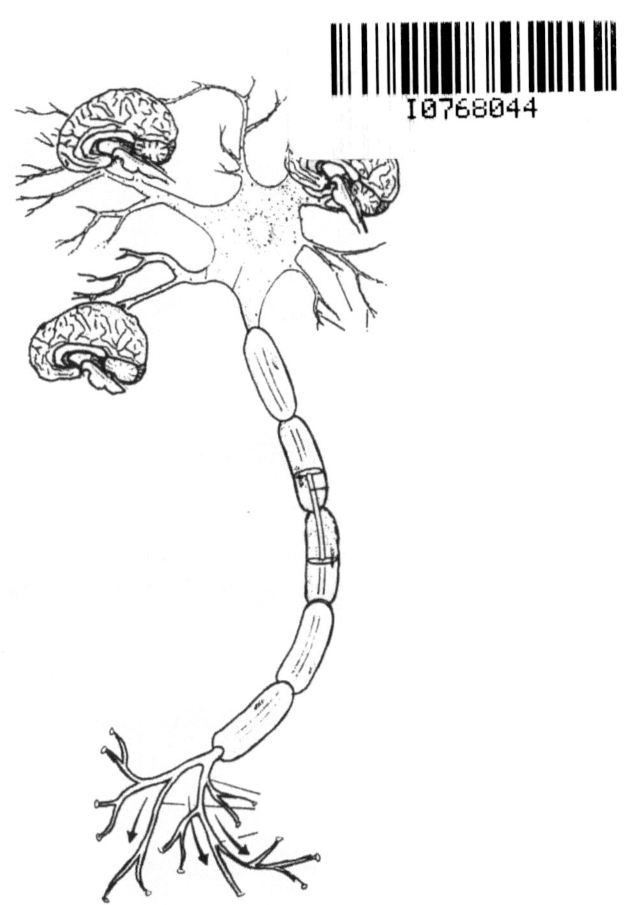

ISSUE 1 – YEAR 1

ISBN: 978-1-968958-00-8

Editor – Jean-Paul L. Garnier

Cover Design – Charles Platt

First Edition | 2025

Space Cowboy Books

61871 29 Palms Hwy.

Joshua Tree, CA 92252

www.spacecowboybooks.com

Table of Contents

Day One

Having owned and operated a bookstore for the last ten years, I'd like to think that I have learned something about readers. There are readers of mainstream fiction, which I will disregard because the bookstore does not cater to these readers, and neither will this magazine. Then there are readers who restrict themselves to specific topics or genres and generally look for books that fall within narrow parameters, titles similar to what they have already read. And lastly, there are my favorite types of readers, those who read like I do – widely, full of curiosity, always looking for something new, something which will break their conceptions of what literature is capable of, and books which redefine the concept of novel. In most cases, modern literature has forgotten the definition of the word "novel" and have stuck to templates of what, and how, a book and its author are expected to operate. While this may sound lofty, language is a technology – one which evolves and alters itself over time. Language belongs to the writer (and reader) to reshape how words and grammar are used, and the very architecture of our minds. For language shapes the way we think, hence programming who we are and how we are capable of thinking.

Because I am of the belief that most readers enjoy sampling a wide variety of texts, I have decided to create a magazine that reflects this infinite variety of what we define as the humanities. I intentionally say humanities because this term excludes so-called "art" created by LLM/AI/generative media. I'll leave that to the tech bros to play with. When inviting contributors, I have asked them for the works that have been stuck in the drawer for lack of appropriate venue, or considered unpublishable due to their lack of clear genre definition. Most artists and authors have these types of works tucked away with nowhere for them to go. Electronic Brain is a home for these works. Electronic Brain will focus not only on texts, but musical scores, pocket dramas, artwork, and any printable material that can fit into the pages of the magazine. It is my belief that the majority of readers are willing to be challenged, are multifaceted, and willing to take a trip through the minds of others. Afterall, reading is a form of telepathy, a direct passage into the mind of another. And our minds are filled with not only words, but music, images, wide varieties of emotion and experience, and so much more. I hope to include science, code, circuit design, cypher, and many other sides of human endeavor. For, as humans, we are also evolving and can choose to do so intentionally. Our arts reflect this, so why not a magazine that does as well? The term "speculative fiction" has always bothered me, because all fiction speculates and asks 'what if' to varying degrees. Likewise, the term "genre" bothers me, because it sets up a series of expectations that are there for marketing and shelving purposes. These terms attempt to put works into tidy little boxes that have very little to do with our internal landscapes. If we considered art and literature as types of food, these classifications would become tiresome almost immediately. "I only eat Italian," for instance, would be a gross oversimplification of the human palate. While preferences are, of course, completely acceptable – wouldn't we want a variety to choose from, to fit our moods and tastes of the moment. With that in mind, I give you Electronic Brain – a magazine which may appeal to fans of speculative fiction (or not), but which also attempts to move the humanities forward, through experiment, unabashed risk taking, and a love of all things new and challenging.

Disagree, agree, have a comment? Send it in and we may print it in the next issue.

Jean-Paul L. Garnier
Joshua Tree, CA
2025

Edging
By Eugen Bacon

Sebu's first fumble is in the undergrowth of the botanical gardens after dark. He's drooled at Clancy from a distance. She's a first year in Philosophy. Things take a turn in the third week of the 12-week course, straight after the "Critical Thinking: Curiosities, Arguments and Logical Fallacies" module with Professor Kazi. Sebu has struggled to find his North Star. Socrates and Aristotle are saying fuck all to him, and it should be a relief—as he collects his shame and frustration into his backpack—when Clancy, the most raven-haired goddess in the tiniest tank top, bare midriffed and baggy army slacks looks him dead straight and says, "You wanna ask me out or what?"

No, he wants to eat her up.

But he doesn't say this.

"We can do… erm…"

"The Brew and Biscuit," she says. "Let's go to the Brew and Biscuit."

"Yeah. OK." His nerves are doing spinal taps on him and his voice sounds like he's pushed his face in a tank of helium.

It doesn't cure his worries when, at the on-campus cafe, Clancy pulls out a loaf of sourdough from her carryall, holds it out to the befuddled waiter, and says, "Do you do BYO bread?"

The girl stammers words that are hedging towards "no," but the pierce in Clancy's gaze makes the waitress accept the loaf and serve it back on a platter, sliced.

"You haven't toasted it," Clancy says.

Out of embarrassment, and because his mother has raised him well, Sebu orders three "dry almond chais" to overcompensate for Clancy's air of entitlement, and because Clancy looks like the type of girl who prefers organic shit.

As the girl writes down his order, Clancy adds, "I'll have a weak, lukewarm soya decaf, one natural sugar."

So, obviously, Sebu drinks all three almond chais by himself, but—through all that stomach bloating and gas releases—Clancy's 120-carat smile makes it worth his while.

There's no light to see in the botanical gardens as Clancy falls onto him. Sebu is swallowed in reaching limbs and untidy tangles stifled in moss. Now Clancy is whipping her tank top off. He touches her naked skin, half-remembers an unfinished song and begins to see mermaids. The sky lifts away and that is that.

Ugghh. Ugghh.

He doesn't even get to unzip his pants.

He opens his eyes to a damp silence and the accusatory glare of violet eyes in the nature requiem of the botanical gardens. The world doesn't eat him up and no hot air balloon swoons down to escort him from shame or the indignant judgement in Clancy's expression as she pulls her tank top back on.

He knows there's a story in there somewhere, just not today.

She doesn't look at him all the way out of the blackened garden, even as a rose quartz moon pushes out of the night to also judge him. Running is impossible, so he coughs, coughs, coughs... but they both know it's unreal.

Did you know? A dingo nearly took you when you were a child, Sebuleni, his mother always said to him. He imagines the wilderness beast stalking him, lunging for the back of his neck, plunging him facedown into the shallow of a running creek as its rank breath of carcasses pushes him deeper into the water so it can drown him then eat him. It doesn't let go even as grown-ups pelt it with stones.

Is that what damaged him?

He unenrolls from Philosophy—stuff logical fallacies, Kafka and Aristotle. He stands behind a wall, a tree, and is reduced to crouching under a desk anytime he sees Clancy within several hundred feet. One noon she comes up to him, bared midriff and all, looks under the campus library table, stares at him deadpan with those zoisite eyes.

"You think I can't see you?"

Cringe. Nearly shits himself.

He feels colder and older than the sky. He knows he'll think this way through the pearl morning light, his heart torn between concern and disbelief. He feels stained—that feeling like he's just buried dog heads.

~

Perhaps he's just discovering himself, that's why he goes to a bar called Jigsaw. It's full of unfinished scenes as he downs Long Island iced teas, death in autumns, frostbytes, mostly loaded with ta-kill-yas. Some of the cocktails smoke or weep topaz rain.

In the tantalising absence of selfhood, he finds the entrance to another trick whose name is Prawn, and there's a right sequence in there somewhere. Perhaps it's a garden or a gate, a sciatica of social interaction, maybe a simple act of affection or spite with a stranger behind a door and there's a stink of comfort, until there isn't—who decides?

He feels dirty about it. There's nothing wrong, per say, with what happened with Prawn at Jigsaw. Well, the kind of "nothing wrong happened" when his father isn't a pastor. Which he isn't. But Sebu didn't feel good about the incident, mostly because he isn't really a one-night-stander. And, sure, he may be bicurious, but he's a bicurious demi, as in demisexual. He read about it, how demis need an emotional connection with a person first, to go all the way. He can't explain how the logic applies to the way things quickly moved with Clancy, until, until—

But he'd fancied her for weeks, if that counts as building an emotional connection. He just wishes there were no unfinished songs or mermaids.

~

He thinks he's done with trying a hand at the relationship thing, but can't explain to himself why he slips into Asantewa's DMs. Maybe it's because he's not too bad at being invisible, well, maybe he is, because Clancy located him under a desk. But one thing leads to another and now he has a GF who permanently lives in his apartment.

"We're mates for life," she says, bouncing on his bed but he's in no doubt how friend-zoned things are looking. He and Asantewa have never gone past a cheek peck although she goes all nuddy, tits out, from the bathroom to the kitchen, and it takes everything for him to contain himself before slipping into a frantic stroke alone in the toilet.

Ugghh. Ugghh.

"Mate, are you wanking?" Asantewa asks from behind the door.

When he finally brings himself to face her, he tries to explain but she doesn't get it, how green he really is.

"What? You never been with a chick?" she says.

Her solution to that whole fiasco with Clancy is a pack of condoms.

The packaging comes with the words that say, "feel everything," "ultra soft," and that's enough to cause calamity to his mortal shame, because people are looking.

Ugghh. Ugghh.

NextGen Skyn burns his back trouser pockets all the way home from the chemists, where Asantewa is waiting for him in a silk negligee. Bugger, the sight of her…

Ugghh. Ugghh.

"What you need is normalization," she says cheerfully, after he's cleaned himself.

~

They climb up many steps into the lacquered floor of a shop named Tantra. Arrayed inside and all the way from the entrance to a backroom are vivacious displays of velvet cufflinks no. 388 and lubes labelled Sensuous, Smooth n Slippery, Fruity Love, Hot 'n' Juicy and Delightful Warming. Sebu refuses to finger the silken face masks, pink with dusky feathers along the edges and won't even look at the red and black whips with shredded lashes because… ugghh, ugghh… he runs to the gents.

They leave Tantra without buying a single thing but Asantewa is all good about it. "Normalization doesn't happen in seconds," she says.

He tries to get over it but has recurring nightmares of silent screaming face down in dirty water, a dingo viciously gripping the back of his neck. When the incident happened, bloody hell, he was a child, the fucken beast didn't even eat him. Just like that, the dingo spat him out. Didn't it like Sebu's taste? Wasn't he good enough for a dingo to eat?

But his mother had another theory.

"The gods love you, Sebuleni. That's why you lived."

No wonder he doesn't live with her anymore.

~

Asantewa visits Tantra alone and brings home Magic Touch. It vibrates and is rechargeable, promises G-spot stimulation, looping orgasms in seconds. She lifts it out of the packaging and…

Ugghh. Ugghh.

This is too much! Sebu is way too ashamed of himself that this keeps happening.

He runs to the bathroom with a cry, turns on the faucet, puts his face in the water and screams. He imagines himself in the deepest blue water out in the open seas. As he lies there, star-eagled, floating in the calm, floating, floating, monstrous eyes approach him, and it's a great white shark. It cycles, cycles him in an s-swim pattern, then a triangular snout turns in a sudden twist, knocks him over, and jaws open wide to reveal serrated teeth. He shrieks as the shark grabs him about the arms and chest, shakes him four times…

~

Asantewa introduces Sebu to edging.

"Edging?" he says.

"It's a holistic level that makes you more keenly aware of your own sexual responses both solo and with a partner."

"What for?" he gasps.

"It's a way of bringing mindfulness into the bedroom."

"Mindfulness?" he repeats unthinkingly.

"But, with you, I think we need one thing more." She refuses to elaborate.

They start with a yawning exercise.

"Stretch to the back of your throat," Asantewa says. "Open your whole mouth and face. Listen to your consciousness. Now relax your jaw, breathe in through the mouth. Ahhhh."

She puts the tips of her fingers on him and he's awake, fully aware and on the brink, when *zinggg*! He shrieks as the taser in her hand throws him out of any unfinished songs or mermaids, no premature flying fish.

They begin to make more progress, first yawning, relaxing jaws, touching… The knowledge that a taser is right there puts the thought of an immediate orgasm right out of his mind. He's lasting 30 seconds, three minutes, 15 minutes, stimulating himself, repeat, and stopping before his body gets a chance to disappoint him with untimely soars to sepulchral cities that leave him with the guilt of burying dog heads.

The dingo that nearly ate him did not damage him.

Edging helps him find the mind to stop cognitive stimulation, waiting about 30 seconds, and then stimulating himself again, repeating until he is ready to go to the next level, which he doesn't.

~

The day Asantewa asks him to lie on top of her, clothed, he edges.

Edging is magical. It floats him on a night sky, drifting around brightly-lit star zones, even as the celestial objects are themselves so very remote. He looks up in wonderment and the stars blink back their astonishment that he's this near yet so far. The night sky isn't black at all, but a radiance of browns, blues, pinks and golds in a kaleidoscopic whirlpool that takes his breath.

He comes to, and there is Asantewa beaming at him with happiness.

She fist-pumps him and says, "See, I told you. Edging is a whole other level."

She doesn't suggest they go all the way.

~

The next evening, Asantewa talks about a backward wheelbarrow, and Sebu feels himself about to hear unfinished songs and see mermaids. As she reaches for the taser, he shakes his head, closes his eyes and thinks of an old woman's bloomers swaying in an outdoor breeze. He puts all his focus on the bloomers—red dotted pettipants, ugly as fuck.

He edges and falls into time and space, even though logic says he's moving upwards into the aura of an amoebic topaz speckled with lilac and golden eggs in the galaxy.

He comes to, and Asantewa is looking at him like a miracle.

"Go you!" she says with pride, slaps him on the back.

~

One day, after the yawning exercises, Sebu stretching to the back of his throat, Asantewa helps him strip. She lies naked on her back on the floor, wraps him with her arms and legs, puts him in a chest lock and he edges… He's in an all-existence and it's unknowably vast, too colossal for his human mind, and he feels alien. It's an out-of-body experience, and he's bounding light-years into the universe where a star-forming nebula starts opening to swallow him up.

Somewhere in the haziness of his mind, he feels tightness and wetness engulfing him, and hears Asantewa's whisper. "Now, Sebuleni."

A spotlight casts on him and he is astounded by explosion after explosion after explosion that surge in eloquent glitters inside his core.

Shock waves shatter him into the brilliance of a brand new star.

James Machell & John Clute - photo by Judith Clute

Cozy Catastrophes - An Interview with John Clute

John Clute is perhaps the most prolific creator of SF-related non-fiction. As a co-founder of The Encyclopedia of Science Fiction and The Encyclopedia of Fantasy, his meticulous analysis has helped shape the way genre literature is understood. And as a co-founder of Interzone, Britan's longest running SF magazine, he has also contributed to its future. His non-fiction is sure-footed but creative, opinionated yet accurate, his reviews and articles having appeared in venues as diverse as New Worlds, New York Times, and The Washington Post. *The Disinheriting Party*, his first novel, was published in 1977 and followed by *Appleseed* (2001) which with its rich vocabulary is a linguistic dance. The Encyclopedia of Science Fiction, having progressed from print through audio, now contains over eight million words of history and analysis.

What first struck me about his home (besides the beautiful art on display thanks to the creative talents of Judith Clute) is the lack of SF books. Besides Gene Wolfe's *The Book of the New Sun*, I noticed comparisons of classic authors, volumes of poetry and history, plus literary criticism, all on dense wall-to-wall bookshelves. John Clute is not a man drawn to fantastika in the way stereotypical SF fans aim to claim ownership over a world (or worlds) vaster than their own. He explores the direction literature has to take once realism is exhausted and contextualizes it within the broader category of the written word. Our conversations have always been illuminating and this one focuses on how SF has changed since the dawn of his career.

James Machell

JM: *How would you describe the SF landscape when you first began to engage with speculative fiction?*

JC: Back in 1950, 1960, the SF landscape and the political landscape and the cultural landscape were not identical, but they were not radically at odds. There was an underlying sense in

American science fiction that the advocacy of a particular kind of future was sort of in cahoots with what people actually secretly or publicly thought.

It was not, at that time, in a state of transgression against the episteme.

JM: *How big a role, do you think, New Worlds played in ending the Silver Age?*

JC: There's... Excuse me, the cough has nothing to do with any kind of cognitive element here. Any kind of ginger movement has an inexorable, inevitable habit of thinking of itself as central, as of importance. It is all about saying and demonstrating something, so it is inherently going to believe that it has done so. And the New Worlds revolution was more like a suffusion of tint in the world. I think what was going on with the Silver Age at that point was that for a variety of reasons in the early 1960s, it was ending. It was breathing fumes, so what New Worlds was basically saying is, "You're breathing fumes."

JM: *Oh, I didn't know that.*

JC: You're basically breathing fumes, but the fumes are poisonous. You're presenting a conservative outmoded, narrow, illiterate vision of the world and of how the world is described. And we are going to change everything. Well, they announced that. That was good enough. An announcement is as good as a kick in the pants.

JM: *When do you think feminist voices in the genre began to be heard and actually identified as feminist?*

JC: I think writers like Joanna Russ were vigorously feminist from the get-go, from when they began to actually write and work. Ursula Le Guin was also much more quietly, but she was very clearly of a mind that there was very powerful need in the science fiction community and in its representation of women for a radical change. She worked from within, Joanna Russ assaulted from without. Many women, because they're human, through the entire century, had felt outraged. Articulation of that just outrage within a frame of understanding that doesn't completely drown it in condescension and refusal and the wrong kind of money.

JM: *Are there any writers in particular whose writing you think brought about a notable shift in the way SF is written?*

JC: What kind of writers are you thinking about?

JM: *Bester would be the first that sprang to mind for me.*

JC: You know, it's easy to think of the Golden Age of Science Fiction as diminishing slowly into a silver age and then being truncated and given the finger by the New Wave. But in fact, it was of course much more complicated than that from the point at which new platforms became available for post-war writers. And I think really what we're talking about is what began to happen around 1950, 51, 52, 53, when Galaxy and The Magazine of Fantasy and Science Fiction was founded, as well as Ace Books and Ballantine Books, all hungry for copy. And the people who were writing that copy in large numbers were people who had a different view of the advocacy of the previous generation.

But that advocacy continued to be the official story. The space race, the outward movement of Homo sapiens, the structure of a space opera as an arena for Homo sapiens to repeat previous triumph – that was always there. I just read a novel by Tom Godwin called *The Survivors*, 1958. And the extraordinary, impossible, archaicness of the story did not come across as jarring, and that was almost 60 years ago, or it's more than 60 years ago, at the time when we weren't conscious of it. Are you conscious every time you go to church that there's something very, very weird about the doctrine?

JM: *Not necessarily.*

JC: So, it was possible to read things that were no longer speaking to anybody's actual experience or expectation or sense of how things should be written without quite noticing you were doing it. Now it's impossible. So now we see more clearly that the world back then, the world of science fiction was exceedingly complicated. And then there were authors like Sheckley, Dick, Bester, and Algis Budrys – a whole slew of them. They were not templates. They were not following the template very precisely. It took a long time for that template to dissolve.
Yeah, that was a rambling answer.

JM: *Great answer.*
There's been a growing trend in SF to depict safe, egalitarian, even cozy futures. Do you think this brings about social change as effectively as dystopian writing?

JC: I think the cozy futures that you were mentioning are less numerous than conspicuous when you see them. It's very, very hard to think of a story written in the last 5 or 10 years or a movie made in the last 5 or 10 years that depicts anything like a cozy future. The cozy catastrophes of the 50s are not, when you actually go back and read them, that cozy.
They were so constructed as to translate what everybody knew was likely to be a terminal disaster, whatever kind of catastrophe it was, nuclear war or in more recent years, the devastations of climate change. It was possible to think of polders, to use a term I've used a lot in encyclopedias, or zones of comfort, or enclaves, which would give one a pastoral alternative to the desolation outside. They didn't have to be a very cheerful pastoral alternative to be hugely more cheerful than the world that we actually do expect for our children, our grandchildren, to have to survive in while cursing us. Cozy catastrophes are our board games.

JM: *And it does strike me that not lot of the cozy hits the mainstream. I see a lot of it in magazines, but not so much in film or TV.*

JC: I don't really read much in the way of short fiction. I should because it's always very good and all that.

JM: *But then I suppose it's also quite forgettable. Please don't ask, "What's an example of great cozy short fiction?" I tend to forget them as soon as I've read them.*

JC: You have a great short story because you don't have to continue to the point where the penny drops. You can see the penny lifting off the page and falling off the edge of the last word, but you don't necessarily have to hear it drop.

JM: *Last question. You've edited the* Encyclopedia of Science Fiction *since its first edition in 1979. How has critical evaluation of SF works developed since that time?*

JC: There have been two or three streams of development. There has been the increase in academic studies of science fiction, which was worthy in intention and perhaps unfortunately became tied into the kind of behaviours, the kind of intellectual behaviours required of teachers, of writers, academic writers, within the institutional circumstances. So, I think what happened was that there was an increasing pressure on people who wrote academically for publication or for tenure about science fiction, to institutionalize that understanding, to represent science fiction after a fashion which seemed to legitimize it through making it sound as though it were a science of understanding, as though the science fiction texts were not imponderable, unanswerable stories, but patterns of extractable themes.

Science fiction, being very vulnerable to that, because science fiction is about various things, (it's world-facing), began to be understood as primarily a set of propositions and solutions. It did not, in the academic world, represent a form of storytelling. The result is that there was a kind of distortion in the actual apprehension of science fiction, in which an eminently good and sane writer like Ursula K. Le Guin would be, because she is so easily paraphrased, would be studied again and again and again. Hundreds and hundreds, probably thousands of academic papers on her. But an author like Gene Wolfe, who is not easily paraphrased, slips through the meshes of the academic. So, the image of science fiction, the representation of science fiction, increasingly over the decades became a caricature, and with the gradual death of humanities industries in the Western world, has become something which is basically a dead end for acute studies and for acute readers. At the same time, between 1960 or so and now, there has been a very fortunate growth in what would be deemed to be amateur, non-academic responses.

There are a lot of people like myself who are not academics, who will not be quoted in academic papers because we do not adhere to peer review and we do not follow certain protocols of presentation. But I think people like myself, (underline like myself), are the actual core narrative of understanding of science fiction and of Fantastica as a whole. A term like Fantastika, which is very loose and baggy, which I've been using since 2007 is a term which will not be found easily assimilable to an academic discourse. Too bad for the academics.

The Encyclopedia of Science Fiction, edited by John Clute and David Langford, with contributions from Brian W Aldiss, Thomas M Disch, and John T Sladek is now offering additional benefits to readers via Patreon.

*

A Wife Manufactured to Order
By Alice W. Fuller

First appeared in The Arena, Vol.13 Issue 2, July 1895

As I was going down G Street in the city of W— a strange sign attracted my attention. I stopped, looked, fairly rubbed my eyes to see if they were rightly focused; yes, there it was plainly lettered in gilt: "Wives made to order! Satisfaction guaranteed or money refunded."

Well! well! does some lunatic live here, I wonder? By Jove! I will investigate. I had inherited (I suppose from my mother) a bit of curiosity, and the truth of the matter was this: now nearing the age of forty, I thought it might be advisable to settle down in a home of my own; but alas! to settle down to a life of strife and turmoil, that would not be pleasant; and that I should have to do, I knew very well, if I should marry any of my numerous lady acquaintances – especially Florence Ward, the one I most admired. She unfortunately had strong-minded ways, and inclinations to be investigating woman's rights, politics, theosophy, and all that sort of thing. Bah! I could never endure it. I should be miserable, and the outcome would be a separation; I knew it. To be dictated to, perhaps found fault with – no, no, it would never do; better be a bachelor and at least live in peace. But – what does this sign mean? I'll find out for myself.

A ring of the bell brought a little white-haired, wiry sort of a man to the door. "Walk in, walk in, sir," he said.

I asked for an explanation of the strange sign over the door.

"Just step right in here and be seated, sir. My master is engaged at present, sir, with a great politician who had to separate from his wife; was so fractious, sir, got so many strange notions in her head; in fact, she wanted to hold the reins herself. You may have seen it – the papers have been full of it. Why, law bless you, sir, the poor man couldn't say his soul was his own, and he is here now making arrangements with master to make him a quieter sort of wife, some one to do the honors of the home without feelin' neglected if he happens to be a little courteous to some of his young lady friends. You see, master makes 'em to order, makes 'em to think just as you do, just as you want 'em to; then you've got a happy home, something to live for. Beautiful – golly! I've seen some of the beautifulest women turned out, 'most make your mouth water to look at." And so the old man rattled on until I was quite bewildered.

I interrupted him by asking if I could see his master.

"Oh, certainly, sir; you just make yourself comfortable and I will let you know when he is through."

I sat for some time like one in a dream, wondering if this could be so, and with many wonderful modern inventions in mind I began to think it possible. And then there was a vision of a happy home, a wife beautiful as a dream, gentle and loving, without a thought for anyone but me; one who would never reproach me if I didn't happen to get home just at what she thought was the proper time; one who would not ask me to go to church when she knew it was against my wishes; one who would never find fault with me if I wished to go to a base-ball game on Sunday, or bother me to take her to the theatre or opera. A man, you know, can't give much time to such things without interfering greatly with his comfort. Oh! could all this be realized? But just then my reverie was broken by the old man, who was saying: "Just step this way. Master, let me introduce you to Mr. Charles Fitzsimmons."

Short, thick-set, florid complexion, pale blue eyes with a sinister twinkle, was the description of Mr. Sharper, whom I confronted. Reaching out his hand, which was cold and clammy and reminded me very much of a piece of cold boiled pork, he said:

"Now, young man, what can I do for you? Want a life-companion, a pleasant one? Man of means, no doubt, and can enjoy yourself; a little fun now and then with the boys and no harm at all – none in the least. When a man comes home tired, doesn't like to be dictated to; want someone always to meet you with a smile, someone that doesn't expect you to be fondlin' and pettin' 'em all the time. I understand it – I know just how it is. Law bless my soul, I've made more'n one man happy, and I've only been in the business a short time, too. Now, sir, I can get you up any style you want – *wax*, but can't be detected."

"Do you mean to say you manufacture a woman out of wax, who will talk?"

"That's just what I do; you give me the subjects you most enjoy talking upon, and tell me what kind of a looking wife you want, and leave the rest to me, and you will never regret it. I will furnish as many 'phones' as you wish; most men don't care for such a variety for a wife – too much talk, you know," and he chuckled and laughed like a big baby.

"What are your prices, may I ask?"

"Well, it's owing a good deal to how they are got up – from five hundred to a thousand dollars."

"Well," I said, "I think that rather high."

"Dear man alive, a pleasant companion for life for a few hundred dollars! Most men don't grumble at all for the sake of having their own way and a pleasant home, and you see she ain't always asking for money." (Sure enough, I hadn't thought of that.)

"Very well, I will decide upon the matter and let you know."

"All right, young man; you'll come back. They all do, them as knows about it."

I went to my room at the hotel and thought it all out, thought of the pleasant evenings I could have with someone whose thoughts were like my own, someone who would not vex me by differing in opinion. I wondered what Florence would say. I really believed she cared for me, but she knew how I disliked so many of the topics she persisted in talking upon. What mattered it to me what Emerson said, or Edward Bellamy wrote, or Henry George, or Pentecost? what did I care about Hume or Huxley or Stuart Mill? any of those sciences, Christian Science or Divine Science or mind cure? – bah! it was all nonsense. The topics of the day were enough, and if I attended closely to my business I needed recreation, not such things as she would prescribe. Still Florence was interesting to talk to, and I rather liked her at times when she talked every-day talk; but I could not marry her, and it was her own fault. She knew my sentiments, and if she would persist in going on as she did I couldn't help it.

Yes, I decided I would have a home of my own, and a wife made to order at once. Before leaving the city I made all necessary arrangements, hurried home, rented a house, and went to see old Susan Tyler, whom I engaged as housekeeper; she was deaf and had an impediment in her speech, but she was a fine housekeeper. All my preparations made, the ideal home! Oh! how my heart beat as I looked around! – what happiness to do as I liked, a beautiful, uncomplaining wife ready to grant every wish and meet me with a smile! What would the boys say when, out a little late at night, I should be so perfectly at ease? I could just see jealousy on their faces, and I laughed outright for joy. To-morrow I was going for my bride. Side-looks and innuendos were thrust at me from all quarters, but I was too happy to demur or explain. When I reached the city I could scarcely wait for the appointed time.

Alighting from the carriage the door was opened, and I was ushered into the presence of the most beautiful creature I had ever beheld. The hands extended towards mine, the lips opened, and a low, sweet voice said, "Dear Charles, how glad I am you have come!" I stood spellbound, and only a chuckle from Mr. Sharper brought me to my senses.

"Kiss your affianced, why don't you?" he said, and chuckled again.

I felt as though I wanted to knock him down for speaking so in that beautiful creature's presence. And then a little soft rippling laugh, and she moved towards me. Oh, could I get that beast to leave the room! Why did he stand there chuckling in that manner?

"Sir," I said, "you will oblige me by leaving the room for a few moments."

With that he chuckled still louder and muttered, "Bless me, I really believe he thinks her alive." Then to me: "To be sure, to be sure, but you only have a short time before going to the minister's, and I must show you how to adjust her. When you get home," –

and he chuckled again – "you can be just as sentimental as you please, but just now we will attend to business. Here are a box of tubes made to talk as you wished them. They are adjusted so. Place the one you wish in your sleeve. You can carelessly touch her right here if there is anyone around. Here is a spring in each hand and the tips of her fingers. I will give you a book of instructions, and you will soon learn to arrange her with very little effort, just to suit yourself, and I am sure you will be very happy. Now, sir, the time is up; you can go to the minister's."

As I put her wraps around her and drew her arm through mine she murmured so sweetly, "Thank you, dear." How glad I was to get out of the presence of that vile man who was constantly pulling or pushing her; I could scarcely keep my hands off from him, and my serene Margurette – for I decided to call her that – would only smile and say, "Thank you!" "Oh, how lovely!" "Ah, indeed!" I was almost vexed with her to think she did not resent it. I wanted her all to myself where I could have the smiles, and thought I should be thankful when we were in our own home.

During our journey I could not help noticing the admiring glances from my fellow travelers, but my beautiful wife did not return any of their looks. In fact, I overheard a couple of young dudes say, "Just wait till that old codger's back is turned, and we shall see whether she will have no smiles for any but him." I had half a notion to adjust her to give them some cutting reply and then go into the smoker awhile, for I was sure they would try to get into conversation with her; but pshaw! I hadn't ordered any tubes of that kind. I believed I'd send and get one in case of an emergency. No, I wouldn't have such in the house; I wanted an amiable wife, and when we were once at home it would not be necessary. I wouldn't *have* to go with her anywhere unless I wanted to. Only think of that! – never feel that my wife would ask me to go with her and I have to refuse, then ten to one have her cry and make a fuss about it. I knew how it was, for I had seen too much of that sort of thing in the homes of my friends.

Business ran smoothly; everything was perfect harmony; my home was heaven on earth. I smoked when I wished to, I went to my base-ball games, I stayed out as long as I pleased, played cards when I wished, drank champagne or whatever I fancied, in fact had as good a time as I did before marriage. My male friends congratulated me upon my good fortune, and I was considered the luckiest man anywhere around. No one knew how I had made the good luck for myself.

There are some things in life I could never understand. One of them is that, when everything seems so prosperous, calamity is so often in the wake. And that was the case with me. After so many prosperous years a financial crash came. I tried to ward it off; I was up early and late. Margurette never complained, but was always sweet and smiling, with the same endearing words. Sometimes as the years went by I felt as though I would not object to her differing with me a little, for variety's sake; still it was best. When I would say, "Margurette, do you really think so?" and I would speak so cross to her often – I don't know but that I did so more than was necessary; still a man must have some place where he can be himself, and if he can't have that privilege at home, what's the use of having a home? – but she was never out of patience, and my wife would only say, "Yes, darling," so low and sweet. I remember once I said, when I was worried more than usual, "I am damned tired of this sort of thing," and she laughed so sweetly and called me her "own precious boy."

But the crash came, and there was no use trying to stay it any longer. I came home sick and tired. It was nine o'clock at night, with a cold, drizzling rain falling. Susan had gone to bed sick, and forgotten to light a fire in the grate. I went into the library, where Margurette always waited for me. No lights; I stumbled over a chair. I accidentally touched Margurette. She put up her lips to kiss me and laughingly said, "Precious darling, tired to-night?" Great God! I came very near striking her.

"Margurette, don't call me darling, talk to me; talk to me about something – anything sensible. Don't you know I am a ruined man? Everything I have got has been swept away from me."

"There, precious, I love you," and she laughed again.

"Did you not hear what I said?" I screamed.

But she only laughed the more and said, "Oh, how lovely!"

I rushed from the house. I could not endure it longer; I was like one mad. My first thought was, where can I go, to whom can I go for sympathy? I cannot stand this strain much longer, and to show weakness to men, I could never do that. I will go to Florence, I said. I will see what she says. Strange I should think of her just then!

I asked the servant who admitted me for Miss Florence.

"She is indisposed and cannot see anyone to-night."

"But," I said, writing on a card hastily, "take this to her."

Only a few moments elapsed and she came in, holding out her hand in an assuring and friendly way. "I am surprised to see you to-night, Mr. Fitzsimmons."

"O Florence!" I cried, "I am in trouble. I believe I shall lose my mind if I cannot have someone to go to; and you, dear Florence, you will know my needs; you can counsel, you can understand me."

"Sir!" Florence said, "are you mad, that you come here to insult me?"

"But I love you. I know it. I love the traits that I once thought I despised."

"Stop where you are! I did not receive you to hear such language. You forget yourself and me; you forget that you are a married man – shame upon you for humiliating me so!"

"Florence, Florence, I am not married; it is all a lie, a deception."

"Have you lost your reason, Mr. Fitzsimmons? Sit down, pray, and let me call my father. You are ill."

"Stop," I cried, "I do not need your father. I need you. Listen to me. I imagined I could never be happy with a wife who differed in opinion from me. In fact, I had almost decided to remain single all the rest of my days, until I came across a man who manufactured wives to order. Wait, Florence, until I have finished – do not look at me so. I am indeed sane. My wife was manufactured to my own ideas, a perfect human being as I supposed."

"Mr. Fitzsimmons, let me call my father." And Florence started towards the door. She was so pale that she frightened me, but I clutched her frantically.

"Listen," I said, "will you go with me? I will prove that all I have told you is true."

My earnestness seemed to reassure her. She stopped as if carefully thinking, then asked me to repeat what I had already told her. Finally she said yes, she would go.

We were soon in the presence of my beautiful Margurette, whom I literally hated – I could not endure her face. "Now, Florence, see," I cried; and I had my wife talk the namby-pamby lingo I once thought so sweet. "Oh! how I hate her!" and I glared at her like a madman. "Florence, save me. I am a ruined man. Everything has been swept away – the last to-day. I am a pauper, an egotist, a bigot, a selfish—"

"Stop!" cried Florence. "You wrong yourself; you are a man in your prime. What if your money has gone, you have your health and your faculties, I guess," (and there was a merry twinkle in her eyes); "the whole world is before you, and best of all, no one to interfere with you or argue on disagreeable topics."

"O Florence! I am punished enough for my selfishness. O God!" and I threw myself on the couch, "were I not a pauper, too, there might be some hope for happiness yet."

"You are not a pauper," said Florence, "you are the master of your fate, and if you are not happy it is your own fault."

"Florence, I can never be happy without you. I know now it is too late."

"Too late – never say that. But could you be happy with me, 'a woman wedded to an idea, 'strongminded'? Why, Charles, I am liable to investigate all sorts of scientific subjects and reforms.

And then supposing I should talk about it sometimes; if it was not for that I might think of the matter. As far as money is concerned, that would have little to do with my actions. Still, Charles, upon the whole I should be afraid to marry the 'divorced' husband of so amiable a wife as your present one is. I, with my faults and imperfections! – the contrast would be too great."

"Florence, Florence," I said, "say no more. All I ask is, can you overlook my folly and take me for better, for worse? I have learned my lesson. I see now it is only a petty and narrow type of man who would wish to live only with his own personal echo. I want a woman, one who retains her individuality, a thinking woman. Will you be mine?"

"I will consider the matter favorably," said Florence, "but we shall have to wait a year, for opinion's sake, as I suppose there are not many who know how you had your late wife manufactured to order."

And we both laughed.

KENT

The Official Carcinogen of Science Fiction

transposing score
duration: yep, 37 seconds

thirty-seven seconds of treachery
a micro-aggression

for flute, clarinet, violin, cello, piano & percussion

rocco harris

Fl.
Bb Cl.
Vln.
Vc.
Vib.
Perc.
Pno.
scratch
tone
ord.
pizz.
arco

tangled up in a mounting tension...
Fl.
B♭ Cl.
Vln.
Vc.
Vib.
Perc.
Pno.

transposing score
duration: 1:11

when the cracked menagerie dances

...dedicated to nora rosemary armstrong

for flute, clarinet, violin & cello

rocco harris

Fl.
Bb Cl.
Vln.
Vc.
arco
pizz.
sul
pont
arco
arco
pizz.
sul
pont

Fl.
B♭ Cl.
Vln.
Vc.
sul pont
ord sul D
sul D
sul D
pizz.
arco
pizz.
sul pont
sul pont
ord
pizz.
arco
pizz.
pizz.
arco

transposing score
duration 22 seconds

emergent properties

...for nova hana holtzman

for flute, clarinet, violin, cello, percussion & piano

rocco harris

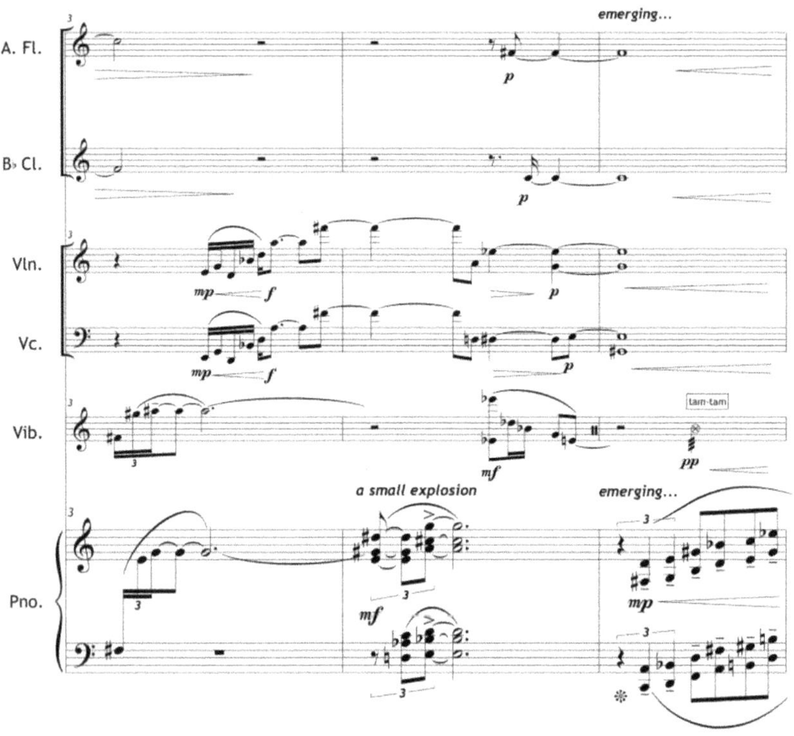

emerging...
A. Fl.
B♭ Cl.
Vln.
Vc.
Vib.
Pno.
tam-tam
a small explosion
emerging...
p
p
mp
f
p
mp
f
p
mf
pp
mf
mp

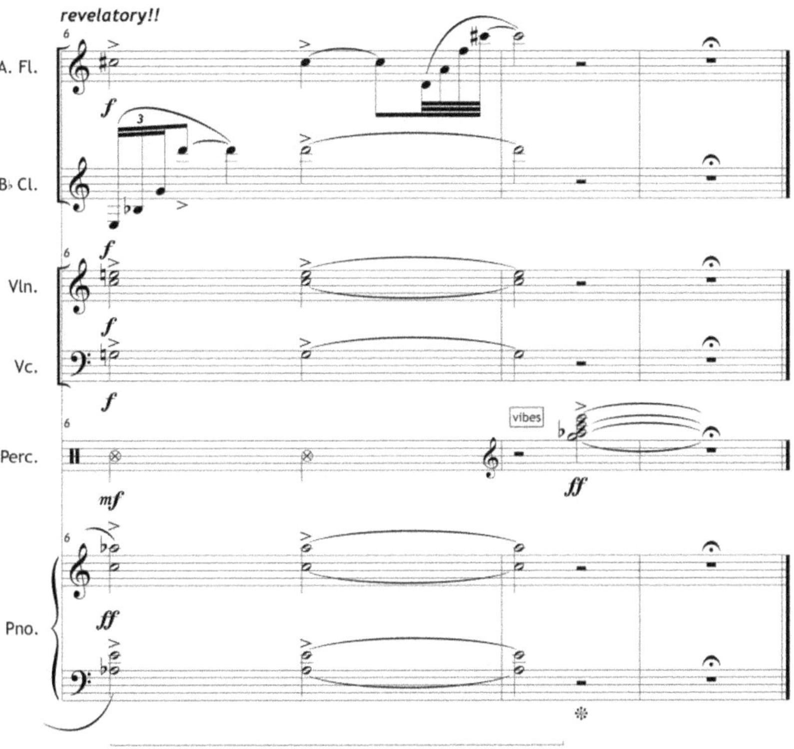
revelatory!!
A. Fl.
B♭ Cl.
Vln.
Vc.
Perc.
vibes
Pno.

transposing score
duration 27 seconds

rather resembling an epiphany

...for hadley laughlin miles

for flute, clarinet, violin, cello & vibraphone

rocco harris

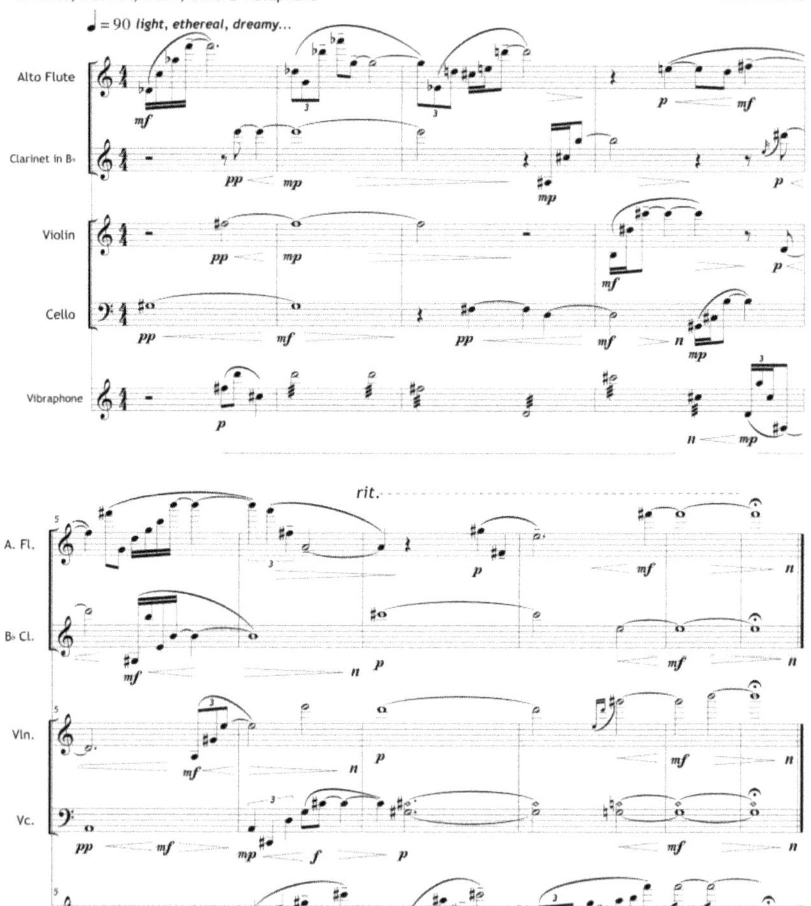

transposing score
duration 23 seconds

strangelet #9

...for everett lincoln kelly

for flute, clarinet, violin, cello, percussion & piano

rocco harris

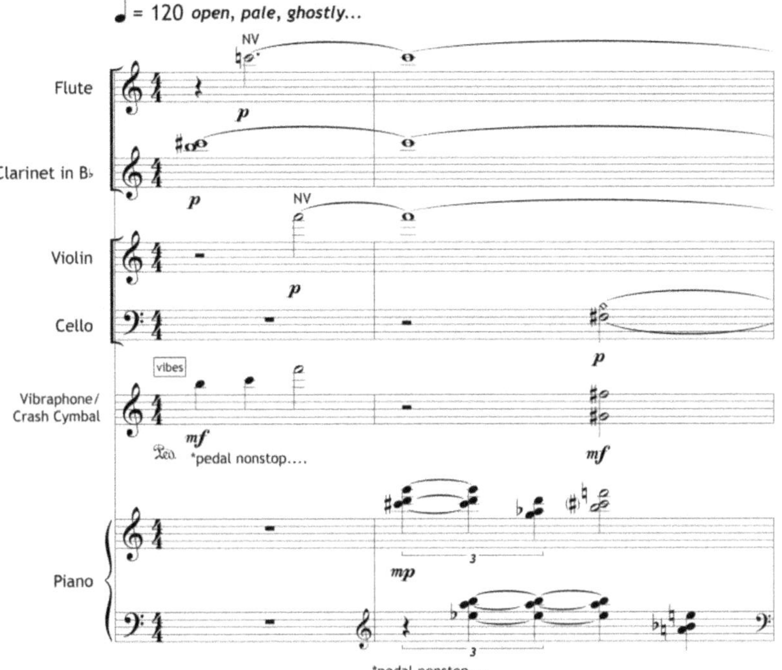

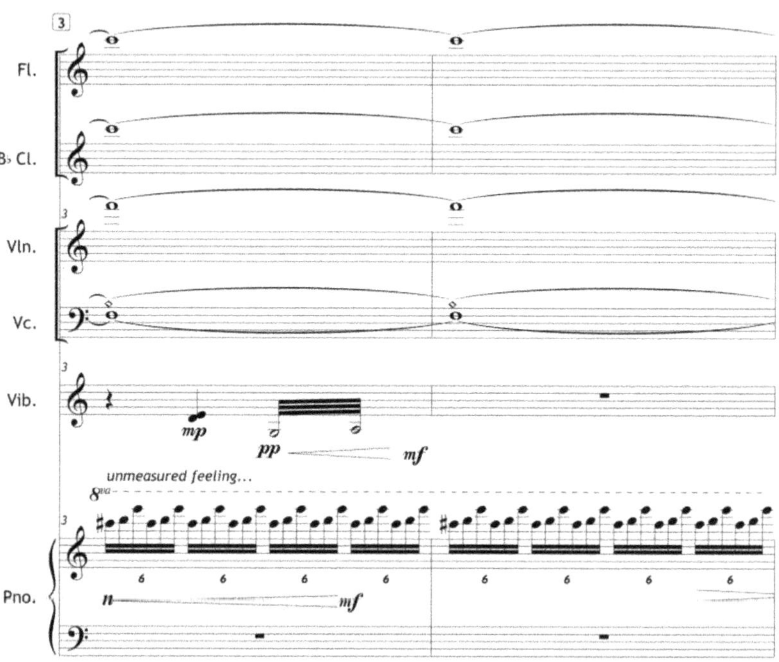
Fl.
B♭ Cl.
Vln.
Vc.
Vib.
mp
pp
mf
unmeasured feeling...
8va
6
6
6
6
6
6
6
6
n
mf
Pno.

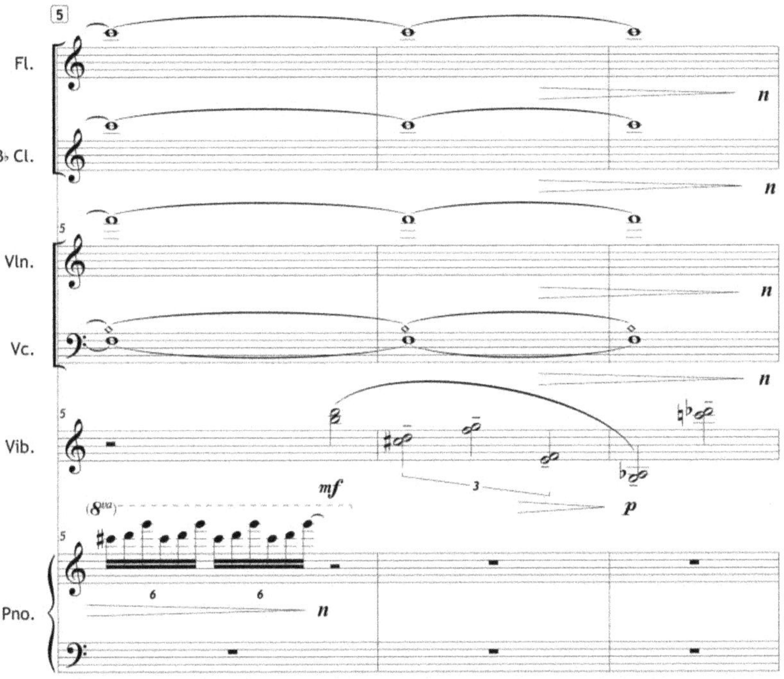
Fl.
B♭ Cl.
Vln.
Vc.
Vib.
Pno.
mf
p
n
(8va)
6   6
5

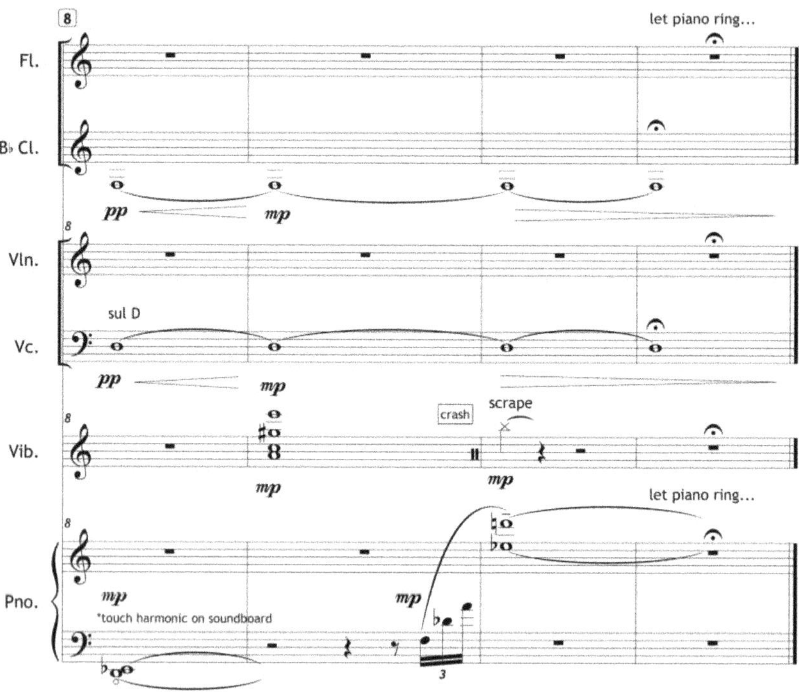
let piano ring...
let piano ring...
Fl.
B♭ Cl.
Vln.
Vc.
Vib.
Pno.
8
sul D
crash
scrape
*touch harmonic on soundboard
pp
mp
pp
mp
mp
mp
mp
mp

transposing score
duration: 1 minute

sympathetic nervous system, part 1: thinking of you

...for nicholas taylor begley

rocco harris

for flute, clarinet, violin, cello, percussion & piano

Fl.
B♭ Cl.
Vln.
Vc.
Vib.
Perc.
Pno.
mf
mf
f
f
f
f
arco
mf
f
f
f
mf
mf
mf
loco
sfz
8vb

Fl.
B♭ Cl.
Vln.
Vc.
Vib.
Perc.
Pno.
pizz.
jete
pizz.
arco
jete
pizz.
arco
pp
mf
mf
pp
mf
pp
mf
mf
pp
mf
mf
pp
mf
mp
sfz
mf
p
f
mp
mf
mf
p
mf
3
3
8vb

Fl.
B♭ Cl.
Vln.
Vc.
Vib.
Perc.
Pno.

Fl.
Bb Cl.
Vln.
Vc.
Vib.
Perc.
Pno.

Fl.
Bb Cl.
Vln.
Vc.
Vib.
Perc.
Pno.

Thomas M. Disch's *AMNESIA RESTORED*
an interview with Gregory Feeley

In 1986 Thomas M. Disch's *Amnesia* was released: interactive "bookware" that landed somewhere between a novel and a video game and was wickedly difficult to play. While this form of entertainment never really caught on, *Amnesia* remains an anomaly in the history of fiction and has now been reprogrammed and rereleased to play for free online. We spoke to Literary Executor Gregory Feeley about the restoration of the bookware and *AMNESIA RESTORED*.

JPG: *What was the catalyst for the restoration of* Amnesia, *and what prompted the decision to make the interactive novel free to the public online?*

GF: When Tom died in 2008, *Amnesia* had been out of print for years. The estate's agent told me that it was utterly out of date and had no commercial possibilities, which was certainly true. I felt that, like other works of Tom's with limited commercial potential (such as his poetry), it should be made available again, but didn't know how to proceed.

Years later, when Mark Bernstein at Eastgate Systems showed interest in republishing the game, Tom sent him the original text and programming notes. Eastgate approached the original publisher, Electronic Arts, but it turned out that EA had not saved the game's source code, which was essentially the game itself. (They had the machine code—what is called the compiled files— but those had been compiled for Electronic Arts' specific technology, and could not be reverted to uncompiled form. All the source code—that is, the creation of the game itself—was gone.)

This meant that anyone who wanted to republish the game would have to create it from scratch, which was too daunting a task for a commercial publisher to undertake for a game that was not likely to sell a lot of copies. So we were stuck for a long time.

And then in 2021 Sarah brought the game to the attention of Dene Grigar, who runs the Creative Media & Digital Culture program in the Department of Digital Technology & Culture at Washington State University in Vancouver. Prof. Grigar is also Director of the Electronic Literature Lab, and she was a big fan of *Amnesia*.

Dene proposed that her senior class undertake, as its semester-long senior project, the full restoration of *Amnesia*. Tom's script was significantly longer than Electronic Arts was able to fit onto a floppy disk, and there was much material EA had not been able to include in the 1986 game. The thirty-two graduating seniors (and four staff members from the Electronic Literature Lab) labored for an entire semester to produce a "complete" version, with modern extra features such as video clips. The account of their heroic efforts (with fascinating visuals) can be read at https://amnesia-restored.com/web/restoration.html

The full results are available at Amnesia-Restored.com, where you can play the "classic" version—the full text, but with an on-screen appearance like the original—or a modernized one. You can also adjust the difficulty level (Tom's version was devilishly difficult to complete without ending up dead, on death row in a Texas prison, or married).

The students who did this had their own Facebook page, and you can find information on the individual members—something of a credits roll—here:

https://www.facebook.com/profile.php?id=100075941361009

JPG: *I've heard that Disch had yet to own a computer when he wrote the initial draft of* Amnesia, *is this true, and if so, how did he handle writing the manuscript in a way that programmers could utilize in the creation of the software?*

GF: I have not been able to establish when Tom first got a computer. There is a 1986 photograph of him holding up a copy of the just-published *Amnesia* at his desk, where you can see an old Kaypro computer with its twin disk drives. My guess is that if Tom did not have a computer when he was commissioned to write the game in 1984 (I had bought my first computer a year earlier), he got one at that point.

JPG: *In the wide breadth of Disch's work, that covers so many styles, genres, and formats, where does* Amnesia *fit in?*

GF: Disch's early novels and stories seemed to obey the unities of place—throughout their stories, the protagonists of *The Genocides* and *Camp Concentration* are "bound in a nutshell" (to quote Disch's favorite play, which he cites repeatedly in his work) and those of *334* or "The Squirrel Cage" or "Descending" were never going anywhere. The pronounced intensity of Disch's early work may owe something to its sense of constraint.

By the time he came to write *On Wings of Song*, however, Disch was willing to send his protagonists out into the world: even, in a sense, to dispatch them upon quests. This sees its apotheosis in *Amnesia*, where the protagonist—penniless and bereft of memory—must venture out into a Manhattan he no longer knows.

More than any of his SF peers, Disch was an author of urban life, and *Amnesia* was his third novel (if that's what it is) to be set primarily in Manhattan. Science fiction tends to be set on frontiers and undiscovered worlds, vistas not yet explored, while genre fantasy remains largely set in romanticized rural landscapes and pre-industrial eras. Disch had little patience with either; his *comédie humaine* was an urban one. His quartet of horror novels are set in Minneapolis, and to the degree that his very last, *The Word of God or, Holy Writ Rewritten*, can be said to have a setting, it modulates between Minneapolis and Manhattan. We know from the notes to *Amnesia* that Disch thought of setting part of the story outside Manhattan; he later thought better. That his interactive novel never leaves the island was utterly in keeping with his art.

Also in keeping was Disch's nameless protagonist as an Everyman rather than a heroic figure. While Disch's contemporaries such as Gordon R. Dickson and David Drake (to name two authors whose books would be found on either side of his in the paperback shelves) gave us protagonists who proceeded from strength to greater strength, showing confidence and proficiency at their tales' beginnings and gaining more as they proceed, Disch declined to engage in such wish-fulfillment. Daniel Weinreb, protagonist of *On Wings of Song*, is pleasant but unremarkable (the novel drives this truth home with merciless clarity), while the Anker family, the main characters in *The Businessman*, are philistine underachievers, more recognizably human than readers might find comfortable.

Will the "you" of *Amnesia*, casting about for clues to his identity, discover that he is a CIA agent with astonishing skills, like Jason Bourne in *The Bourne Identity*, or even an outright superman as in an A.E. van Vogt novel? The game's original players may have wondered, but those who knew Disch's work would have been in no doubt as to the answer.

JPG: *What were Disch's hopes for* Amnesia *and the future of interactive fiction?*

GF: Tom believed that *Amnesia* represented an example of a new art form—"although," he added, "an embryonic specimen." He realized that there would be more such works, with greater complexity and interactivity. I do not know whether he would have continued to work in this form, as Tom was finally a prose (and verse) writer, and you don't get many sentences, let alone lines of poetry, in a computer game.

JPG: *What distinction, if any, did Disch and the developers of* Amnesia *make between an interactive novel and video games?*

GF: They called it "a text adventure," which suggests that they were not sure where its natural audience, or what its actual genre, would prove to be.

JPG: *How did you become the Literary Executor of the Thomas M. Disch Estate?*

GF: I had known Tom since the late 1970s, and he knew that I was familiar with his work and held it in high regard. He had originally named a writer close to his own age as Executor, but then realized that he should actually name someone younger, who would outlive him by many years.

JPG: *What upcoming plans does the Estate have for the publication of Disch's work, and are there any plans to publish the original manuscript of* Amnesia*?*

GF: The original text of *Amnesia*, along with much other material, is available in book form, as *Total Amnesia*. This generous volume was edited and published by Sarah Smith, and runs to 582 pages. You can buy it online from many venues—although I hope you do not use Amazon.

https://amnesia-restored.com

Ghosts
By Michael Butterworth

The Bomb explodes

Because of the emptiness,

The land shrinks

From a fiery breath

And once again

There is only the calm and the quiet of space

Lapping at the Earth

Like a great and timeless sea,

Only a thin and lifeless chill

That blows on the land

As it used to be.

Reason says

That I stand alone,

Listening to this wind,

Comprehending this new wasteland,

But I feel inchoate,

A limb without means.

There can be no person

Such as I

Only the chance

Projections from the past

That bob up and down

On the wind

Too frightened to endure,

No man to appreciate

The futility

Of life lost

After so much

By those who tried to fathom

The hard beauty of the stars ...

No other

To walk in admiration

Of man's fleeting majesty,

For the stars are too far.

The flesh will destroy itself

Wherever it springs.

There can now

Only be truth,

A harsh

Unperceived beauty of matter,

Glimpsed yet unglimpsed

During mankind's life,

A glorious peepshow beyond death

To which all men have striven
And at last achieved.

A phantom housewife
Complete with apron,
Brush, and crying child
Appeared before me
Despairingly
In the air.
'I tried to do my best,
And suckle up to my husband
And bring up our son.
It was my husband
Who never played true,
Who made my life an agony
From beginning to end
And took my mind
Off what I really wanted to do –
My real aim in life
Was to be a model,
A glamour girl
Who all men would love,
Who could rule all eternity.

I would have stopped the war

And saved the world from this.'

She fled with

Her struggling child,

Impelled by the wind,

Her form weaker now

And less able to exist,

But her bit had been said

And her last role

Played out to its utmost.

A car worker took her place

His ghostly skin dulled

And listless,

But his eyes aglint

With a final energy.

'I worked fucking hard

Fixing panels to chassis

Day after day

Stinking with sweat

And fouling my lungs

With metal dust.

The noise of the line

Was never out

Of my ears.

The monotony

Drove me mad. I never

Wanted to do

That God-awful job

In the first place,

But with a wife and kids

What can you do

But buckle down?

What I wanted to be was

A player on the pitch.

I was good at rugger,

But after I got married

Somehow there was never the time.

I got more interested

In getting my wage rise

Than watching what was happening.'

The man belched

And farted

And he too began fading,

Joining the spore of particles

Left behind by the woman.

A novelist appeared next,

His hair long and wild,

His body tall and lean,

Still with the clothes he wore

On the day he died.

He opened both his arms

In a gesture of despair

And shook his head.

'Of course I saw it all coming.

I warned the world in advance

But no one listened.

During my life I achieved what I wanted to,

One of the lucky ones I suppose,

But only at great expense

To my family and others.

Nevertheless I was able

To tour the world

Having a quiet word

In everyone's ear,

And I put in my bit

To save you all.'

Still shaking his head

But looking faintly happy now

He was carried away

On the wind, papers

Streaming from his arms,

The useless efforts

Of his life's work.

A farmer pulled-up

In the cab of his tractor,

Its engine shimmering

And roaring, as though real.

His lips were pursed

In tight amusement,

But his head was sunk with restrained anger

And his eyes stared frozenly from their sockets.

'I too knew what was going on.

How could I ignore it

When my fields were withering

From insecticides

And my soils turning

To fertiliser dust?

My animals were cruelly treated

To make ends meet.

I was forced into a position

In which I never wanted to find myself.

What I wanted was

To be at one

With the Earth,

To enrichen its soil

Not to strip it,

But the pigs

In the cities,

The hungry bastards,

Ate everything

Faster that I could produce it

And still wanted more.

In the end I took my kerosene

To the cities to burn them down,

But by then it was too late.'

He shook his fists at the sand clouds

In a sudden last expression

Of his reasonable body,

Then he turned back to his controls

And revved quickly away,

Depriving the wind of its part.

An economist appeared,

Laughing loudly

And shaking all over

With his nerves.

He wore a suit

And a gold clock

Strapped to his wrist

That he consulted

To keep informed

Of elapsed time.

'Ha! You *would*

Like to blame me!

But I can tell you

With all honesty

I knew nothing!

My system was sound

And my advice given in good faith.

I practiced all my life

To make sure that I became

A man of the world

Before giving you my secrets.

I always wanted to be

What I was.

I loved my job
And I'm sorry now
That we can't all be around
To continue …'
A silken scarf
Which he had been
Carrying to wipe his brow
Fluttered by him in the wind
And gagged on his mouth,
Muffling the final words
He wanted to say.

An industrialist
Trod the empty spot
Looking warily about him
As he spoke.
'I never wanted to be an industrialist.
I wanted to be a poet
And soar on high
Taking the whole human race
With me. But
I was no good with words
And the words I did produce

Never gave me a proper income.

I was forced to prostitute

What little talent I possessed

And go into the Business.

I was unhappy, and lonely,

But as I rose higher

I eventually began to

Reach the limits I had set myself

As a poet, and for a while

I grew happy with my lot.

But instead of elevating

My fellow men

I left them

Blind and purposeless,

And I must confess

That it might have been I

Who conferred with colleagues

And international governments

And unwittingly created

The conditions that

Have led to this.'

Frightened and cowed

His visage was torn apart

By a sudden, unexplained

Fury in the wind

And his ghostly fragments

Were spun away

Into space.

A politician

Reluctantly

Appeared,

Smiling and then frowning,

At first speechless,

And dressless, his words

Find no sure direction,

His clothes no occasion,

But eventually he spoke, and

As he did, the Earth trembled

And shook. Gaping cracks

Appeared in the desert.

Mountains tumbled down

Behind him, and when he

Had finished his brilliant oratory

Applause soared from behind the sky

In a continuous, beating thunder

That echoed round

The globe, sounding his curtain.

Then the cleansing wind

Gathered his protesting form

On its way.

Next came a holy man – a priest, an imam, a

Rabbi,

Smoothing down

His apparel, and holding up

A single finger

To command attention

From the whistling sand.

'It was I

Who conferred with brothers

And believers

Around the world

In our grief and anger

Who brought down Gomorrah.

In the Bible, the Torah,

The Koran

Was it not said that

Jesus, the Messiah, Mohammad

Will reign again?

And finally, in the debris,
A virgin ballerina appeared,
Her sure, white legs extended
And her graceful arms
Curved above her arched spine.
She trilled on her toes
Before gracefully launching herself
Across the sand,
Her ghost the last
And most difficult to depart
As she carried all men and women,
All ages
And all promise of the future,
Away,
In her movement.

There can be no plea
For vanity,
Only pale, mental residues,
Shadows of a former life.
And only these ghosts,

The striven memories of men,

Can find a purpose in the wind,

Carried around the globe

In storms of dust,

Chattering and arguing

About the rights and wrongs –

The echoes of a past

That will never finally fade

But will always travel outwards through space

Long after the Earth herself

Has crumbled

And the stars

Have rearranged.

THIS IS A PROGRAMMED COMIC STRIP. START AT FRAME ONE. YOU HAVE THE CHOICE OF GOING FROM THERE TO FRAME TWO OR FRAME THREE. IF YOU CHOOSE THREE, GO STRAIGHT TO IT, OMITTING FRAME TWO ALTOGETHER.

YOU HAVE A NEW CHOICE, IN EACH FRAME. EVERY TIME YOU CHOOSE A NUMBER, GO STRAIGHT TO IT, OMITTING OTHERS IN BETWEEN.

THERE ARE FOUR ENDINGS. IN THREE OF THEM, NORMAN LOSES HIS STRUGGLE AGAINST AMERICA. BUT IN ONE OF THEM, NORMAN SUCCEEDS.

YOUR AIM IS TO MAKE CHOICES WHICH YOU THINK WILL BE MOST LIKELY TO LEAD NORMAN THROUGH TO THE HAPPY ENDING.

IN ALL, THERE ARE 67 DIFFERENT PATHS THROUGH THE COMIC. THEY VARY IN LENGTH FROM FIVE TO NINE FRAMES. OF ALL THE 67, ONLY 16 LEAD TO SUCCESS, RICHES AND HAPPINESS FOR NORMAN. NOW TURN TO FRAME ONE→

NORMAN WAS AN ENGLISH LAD WHO HAD COME TO NEW YORK TO SEEK HIS FORTUNE....
1
WAP!
RIDE YEL
RIDE SAF
KEEP YOU DISTANCE
HERE I AM — NEW YORK, WHERE STREETS ARE PAVED WITH GOLD, AND BUILDINGS ARE SO TALL THEY TOUCH THE CLOUDS! NOW, SHALL I ② BECOME A STUDENT REVOLUTIONARY? ③ JOIN THE SILENT MAJORITY?
10.70

NORMAN WENT TO A NEARBY UNIVERSITY...
2
HOW DO YOU DO? I'M INTERESTED IN DESTROYING THE OPPRESSIVE FORCES OF THE FASCIST ESTABLISHMENT. CAN I HELP IN ANY WAY?
FAR OUT! MY NAME'S JOE. COME WITH ME, AND
4 SHOPLIFT FROM MACY'S IN OUR PLAN TO UNDERMINE THE MATERIALIST BOURGEOISIE!
5 GET YOUR HEAD STRAIGHT AT THE LOCAL ROCK MUSIC FESTIVAL

AT A NEARBY CONSTRUCTION SITE:
3
EXCUSE ME — I WANT TO JOIN THE SILENT MAJORITY, AND WAS WONDERING...
6 I'M GONNA CRACK YOUR SKULL, SMART-ASS HIPPIE WEIRDO!
7 HEY — IZZAT AN ENGLISH ACCENT?! WHY'N'CHA COME BACK T'MY PLACE, KID, SO I KIN SHOW YA HOW A REAL AMERICAN LIVES!
MOTHER

UNFORTUNATELY, NORMAN'S NEW FRIEND BETRAYED HIM TO THE POLICE! HE WAS THROWN INTO JAIL....
4
NO SPITTI
I FEEL REAL BAD ABOUT IT, NORM! BUT WHEN THE PIGS SHOWED UP, SOMEONE HAD TO TAKE THE RAP. WHEN YOU'VE SERVED YOUR TIME, THOUGH, WE CAN USE THE BREAD I COPPED TO
8 BUY A CAR AND DRIVE TO SAN FRANCISCO
14 GET INTO THE PORNOGRAPHY BUSINESS & HIT IT BIG!
5
AT THE FESTIVAL NORMAN MET JOE'S SISTER, VALERIE — THERE WAS A DEEP RAPPORT...
WHATEVER YOU THINK IS BEST, JOE.
NORMAN, YOU'RE EVERYTHING I'VE BEEN SEARCHING FOR!
4 CHARGING ENTRANCE MONEY TO THIS FESTIVAL IS A BUMMER — YOU CAN HELP ME & JOE RIP OFF THE ORGANIZERS & GIVE THE BREAD TO THE PEOPLE!
9 LET ME TAKE YOU AWAY FROM ALL THIS — MY DAD HAPPENS TO BE A MILLIONAIRE. MARRY ME AND WE'LL LIVE IN LUXURY!
LOVE
PEACE
HMM! THAT SOUNDS A SENSIBLE IDEA.

THE CONSTRUCTION WORKER'S VICIOUS BLOW DAMAGED NORMAN'S BRAIN! HE BECAME A TWITCHING VEGETABLE IN THE GARDEN OF HUMANITY....
6
HAVE ANOTHER, ON THE HOUSE, BUDDY! I LOVE TA HEAR THAT GODDAMN ENGLISH ACCENT — YOU SPEAK IT LIKE IT'S WRITTEN!
TH... THANKS! P... PARDON MY AS... AS... ASKING, BUT I'M LOOKING FOR A J. JOB ....
TREMBLE
OH, YEAH? WELL, WITH YOUR, UH, DISABILITY, YOU OUGHTA TRY
10 MUGGING PEOPLE
11 TAXI DRIVING. HA HA HA! HEY, WATCH WHERE YOU'RE SPILLIN' THAT DRINK, WILLYA?

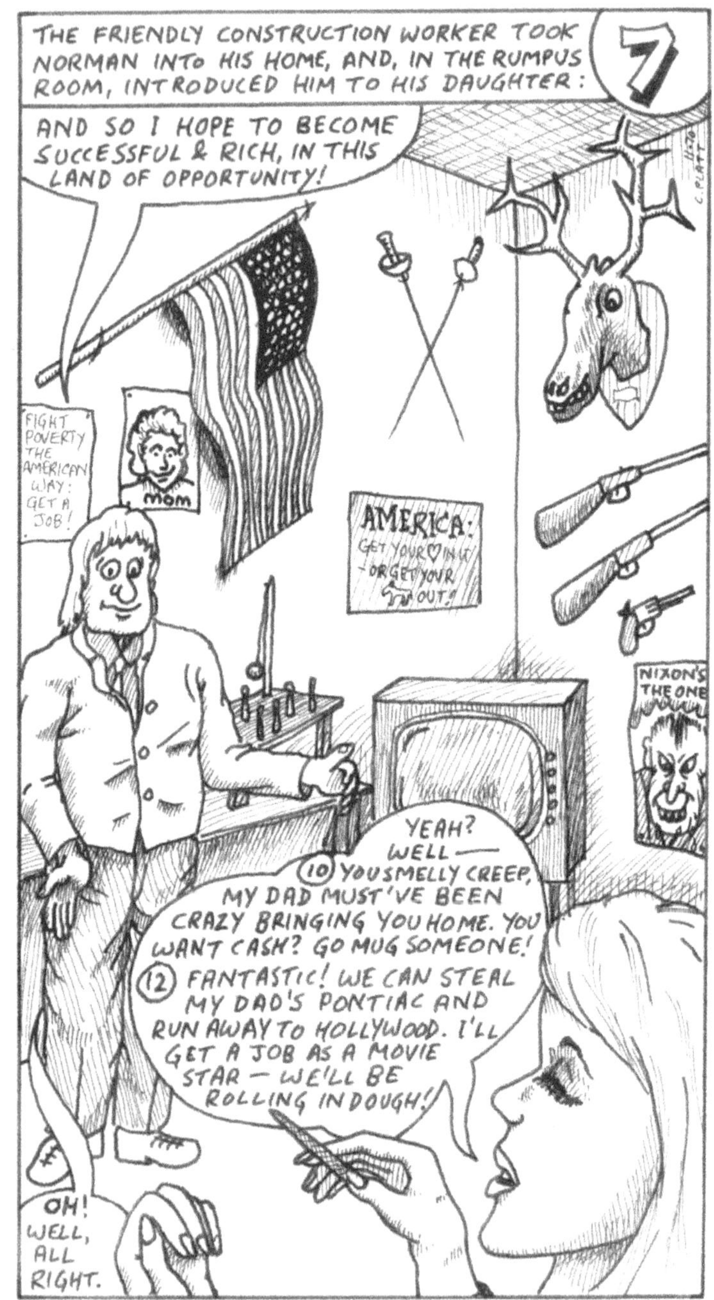

THE FRIENDLY CONSTRUCTION WORKER TOOK NORMAN INTO HIS HOME, AND, IN THE RUMPUS ROOM, INTRODUCED HIM TO HIS DAUGHTER:
7
AND SO I HOPE TO BECOME SUCCESSFUL & RICH, IN THIS LAND OF OPPORTUNITY!
C. PLATT
FIGHT POVERTY THE AMERICAN WAY: GET A JOB!
MOM
AMERICA: GET YOUR ♡ IN IT — OR GET YOUR OUT!
NIXON'S THE ONE
YEAH? WELL — ⑩ YOU SMELLY CREEP, MY DAD MUST'VE BEEN CRAZY BRINGING YOU HOME. YOU WANT CASH? GO MUG SOMEONE! ⑫ FANTASTIC! WE CAN STEAL MY DAD'S PONTIAC AND RUN AWAY TO HOLLYWOOD. I'LL GET A JOB AS A MOVIE STAR — WE'LL BE ROLLING IN DOUGH!
OH! WELL, ALL RIGHT.

SO, TOGETHER, THEY HEADED WEST.
SOME DAYS LATER, IN A TOWN IN ARIZONA:
8
SHEL
white plain
motel
FOOD
GOOD
FOOD
TEX 66
DRIVE-IN BURGER
DECISIONS, DECISIONS! DO WE EAT AT 12 THE 'POST HOUSE' OR 13 HOWARD JOHNSONS ?
EATS

VALERIE MADE THE ARRANGE-
MENTS. SOON SHE & NORMAN
WERE HAPPILY MARRIED! BUT:
SO NOW I'M A MEMBER OF THE SILENT MAJORITY, AFTER ALL. BUT WE'RE IN DEBT, VALERIE IS SPENDING TOO MUCH TIME WITH HER ANALYST FOR MY LIKING, THE DISHWASHER CAUGHT FIRE, THE COLOR T.V. PICTURE IS TOO STRONG ON RED, AND I'M FEELING VERY DEPRESSED. I THINK I'LL
(12) GO ON A VACATION
(14) THROW IT ALL UP AND BECOME A DILDO MANU-FACTURER!
9

IT SEEMED GOOD ADVICE. SO NORMAN TRIED IT!
EXCUSE ME, MISS — I'M A STRANGER HERE IN NEW YORK, A BIT SHORT OF MONEY. I WAS WONDERING IF YOU'D MIND....
10
(9) YOU POOR LOST SOUL! PUT YOUR KNIFE AWAY. I'LL GIVE YOU ALL I HAVE. MOREOVER, I'D BE HAPPY TO MARRY & LOOK AFTER YOU! MY NAME'S VALERIE — COME HOME WITH ME.
(19) MALE CHAUVINIST MOTHERFUCKER! — I'M GOING TO CASTRATE YOU WITH THE CAN OPENER I ALWAYS CARRY FOR SITUATIONS LIKE THIS!
REALLY? OH WELL — WHAT HAVE I GOT TO LOSE?
UPTOWN LOCAL
SUBWAY TIME
WALK—DON'T RUN USE HANDRAILS
NEDICKS ORANGE DRINK
GUM

NORMAN TOOK THE KIND BARTENDER'S ADVICE AND BECAME A CAB DRIVER. BUT, ONE NIGHT...
11
ALL RIGHT, BUDDY! (8) MY NAME'S JOE — PLEASED TO MEET YOU! I'M HI-JACKING THIS YELLOW CAB TO SAN FRANCISCO! (19) I'M A NO-GOOD HIGHSCHOOL DROP-OUT —MY MOM WAS RAPED BY A CAB DRIVER & I'M GONNA CASTRATE EVERY DRIVER IN NEW YORK, TO GET MY REVENGE!
PULL DOWN YOUR PANTS!
HMM ...... I SUPPOSE I HAVE NO CHOICE!
TAXI
ACME CAB CORP

12
THE CAR JOURNEY WENT WELL UNTIL, STRICKEN BY CHRONIC STOMACH PAINS CAUSED BY A MEAL AT A "POST HOUSE" RESTAURANT, NORMAN LOST CONTROL AND A MASSIVE PILE-UP ENSUED.....
YIKES! WHAT A TERRIBLE ACCIDENT! BUT LUCKILY I HAVE BEEN THROWN CLEAR— 16 MY SPINE IS INJURED— I CAN SEE I AM IN FACT THE ONLY SURVIVOR. BUT LOOKS LIKE I'LL BE A HUNCHBACK FOR LIFE! 19 I'VE BEEN —OUCH!— CASTRATED BY THE REAR-VIEW MIRROR!

POWELL & MASON STS
I'M GOING TO BUY SOME UNDERGROUND COMIX, AND SEE A DIRTY MOVIE. IF YOU TAKE MY ADVICE, YOU'LL GO AND 20 JOIN A COMMUNE 21 BECOME A DRUG-PUSHER. SO LONG!
CHEERIO, JOE! I'LL DO AS YOU SUGGEST.

AND SO, EVENTUALLY, NORMAN BECAME A SUCCESSFUL DILDO MANUFACTURER!
14
BUT, ONE DAY SEVERAL MONTHS LATER:
AGH! WHO CAN THIS STRANGE INTRUDER BE? (16) A CRAZED, HOMICIDAL DISSATISFIED CUSTOMER, COME TO BEAT ME UP IN REVENGE FOR A NASTY EXPERIENCE WITH ONE OF OUR COMPANY'S DILDOES? OR, (15) THE MAILMAN?
PATENTS:
MODEL BA
NOTE:
SPECIFICATI
UNITED DILDOES INC.
C. PLATT

THE MAILMAN BROUGHT BAD NEWS —
15
16
YIKES! THE PHONE COMPANY HAS TRACKED DOWN ALL THE LONG-DISTANCE CALLS I MADE WITH MY FAKE CREDIT CARD NUMBER. THEY WANT $10,000!! I'LL HAVE TO (17) GO TO VEGAS, TO WIN THE MONEY (18) ABSCOND, AND BECOME A PENNILESS BUM.
WOUNDS FROM THE ENCOUNTER MADE NORMAN AN INCURABLE HUNCH-BACK! HE SEARCHED FRUITLESSLY FOR A JOB, UNTIL, EVENTUALLY, HE BECAME A FLOOR-SWEEPER ON THE SET OF A MOVIE-DOCUMENTARY ABOUT WEST COAST COMMUNES....
WHAT LUCK! THE STAR OF THE MOVIE — BY COINCIDENCE, A HUNCHBACK SIMILAR TO MYSELF — HAS COME DOWN WITH MALIGNANT CANCER! THIS COULD BE MY BIG BREAK!
DIRECTOR
MAKE A NOTE OF THIS, DOLORES — I'M GOING TO (17) SCRAP THE WHOLE MOVIE AND MAKE EVERYONE UNEMPLOYED! (20) TRY TO CARRY ON, WITH THAT FLOOR-SWEEPER IN THE STARRING ROLE!
L. PLATT 11-70

ALONE & PENNILESS, NORMAN'S ONLY HOPE WAS TO STRIKE IT RICH AT LAS VEGAS....
I'VE WON $7,000! BUT IT'S NOT ENOUGH. I'M GOING TO PUT IT ALL ON 18 BLACK — A SOBER CHOICE. 21 RED — AND DEVIL MAY CARE!
17

Howard Johnsons
18
HEY, KIDS! ALL THE CHICKEN C YOU CAN EAT FOR $1.59!!
TOO BAD! NORMAN'S DECISION LED HIM TO TOTAL FINANCIAL RUIN!
AND SO, FIVE HOURS LATER
I'M DOWN TO MY LAST $2. I MAY AS WELL EAT MYSELF TO DEATH!
BLAM
THE END

AFTER THAT, NORMAN FOUND LIFE RATHER LACKED A SENSE OF PURPOSE. HE SETTLED DOWN AS A NEW YORK BUM, HAUNTING THE PORNOGRAPHY STORES, MOLESTING YOUNG CHILDREN AND USING MIRRORS ON HIS SHOES' TOE-CAPS TO STARE UP GIRLS' SKIRTS IN THE NEW YORK PUBLIC LIBRARY. THEN, ONE DAY...
19
YIKES! THE WALK/DON'T WALK SIGNAL WAS WRONG! I'M DOOMED!
THE END

FOR A WHILE, NORMAN DID WELL IN HIS NEW "RÔLE" AS COMMUNE-MEMBER. HE FOUND THAT "ACTING THE PART" CAME NATURALLY. BUT, ONE DAY, WHILE ON COOKING DUTIES.....
20
MMM! THIS STEW I'M COOKING SMELLS GOOD. I... ERK! I SEEM TO HAVE TRIPPED, AND CAN SEE I'LL FALL INTO THE GIANT CAULDRON! I'LL BE BOILED ALIVE!!! ≥HELP!≤
MUCH LATER:
SAY WHAT YOU LIKE ABOUT OLD NORMAN — HE'S SURE GOT WHAT IT TAKES WHEN IT COMES TO MAKING A REAL FINE STEW!
THE END
C. PLATT 12-70

A WISE CHOICE!
IT GAVE NORMAN ENOUGH MONEY TO INVEST IN REAL ESTATE; INSIDE OF A YEAR, HE WAS A MILLION- AIRE! HE SETTLED DOWN TO LIVE THE AMERICAN DREAM FOR THE REST OF HIS LIFE!
21
THE END.

NORMAN'S Flow DIAGRAM
SHOWING HOW FRAMES IN THE STORY ARE LINKED BY READERS' CHOICES (REPRESENTED BY ARROWS)
START →
HAPPY ENDING →
* NOW YOU CAN PLOT YOUR OPTIMUM PATH!
1
3
2
7
6
5
10
11
4
9
19
14
12
8
15
16
13
17
20
18
21

Interview with Dr. Phoenix Alexander - Jay Kay and Doris Klein Science Fiction Librarian

Photo by Stan Lim, UCR

The Eaton Collection of Science Fiction & Fantasy at University of California Riverside is a rich repository of science fiction history, a place so layered with treasures that it is overwhelming on first visit. Filled with books, ephemera, fandom materials, and so much more, it is a place for research and an amazing asset to those who wish to dive into the history of a genre. We spoke to curator Phoenix Alexander about the collection and his work within this incredible special collections library.

JPG: *Please give us a brief history of the Eaton Collection at UCR?*

PA: The Eaton Collection of Science Fiction & Fantasy is one of the world's largest, richest, and deepest collections of science fiction, fantasy, horror, utopian literature and related genres. The collection originated with the library of Dr. J. Lloyd Eaton: about 7,500 hardback editions of science fiction, fantasy and horror from the nineteenth to the mid-twentieth centuries, which was purchased by the UCR Library in 1969.

The first Eaton Curator was George Slusser, who grew the collection over two decades, and programmed the legendary 'Eaton Conference' series (starting in 1979) that brought together SF scholars and authors. The next conference is taking place at UCR, April 4th-5th! JJ Jacobson was the first named Jay Kay and Doris Klein Librarian for Science Fiction and Fantasy, following the finalization of the Jay K. Klein Endowed Fund for the Support and Preservation of Science Fiction and Fantasy Collections of the UCR Libraries in 2014. Today, the collection has grown to more than 300,000 items, and I have been in my current role as Klein Librarian since 2022.

JPG: Tell us a bit about your background and what led you to the Eaton?

PA: I've had quite a meandering professional trajectory!
I always loved drawing and writing as a kid, and I decided to pursue Fashion Design after leaving high school. I got my degree in Fashion with Print (which combined fashion and textile design) From Central Saint Martins, University of London, before turning back to academia. I completed a second BA, and MA, in English Literature from Queen Mary, University of London.
By that time I had gravitated towards what we might call 'speculative' or even surrealist literature; not SF per se, but genres that experimented with form and structure. I completed my Ph.D. in English and African American Studies at Yale University, writing on the long history of Afrofuturism. At this time I discovered the amazing world of special collections, and worked in the Beinecke Library with brilliant mentors for the last three years of my degree.

By the time I graduated in 2019, my interests in SF, literature, and libraries had all converged, and my first job was as the Science Fiction Collections Librarian at the University of Liverpool, which holds Europe's largest cataloged collection of SF and fantasy. UCR's Eaton Collection is world-famous, and of course I had my sights set on it—although I did have to wait a few years to apply, due to the COVID-19 pandemic.

JPG: *What are some of the specialties of the Eaton, and what types of research are conducted at the collection?*

PA: All sorts! What's so exciting about working here is that you really do get to meet people from all over the world, doing all sorts of projects: from UCR undergrads and grad students in classes as diverse as English, Art History, Physics, and Political Science, to postdocs, visiting artists, and film-makers. Last year I worked with PBS on two documentaries (one on Judy-Lynn Del Rey, which you can view online, and the other forthcoming early 2026).
 The Eaton Collection has strengths in SF periodicals and 19th and 20th-century Anglophone SF in particular, as well as exhaustive collections on US-based fandom, through collections from Fred Patten, Bruce Pelz, and many others. We have film and television scripts—including an extensive collection on Star Trek and K/S slash fanzines—and huge archival collections from some of the most iconic editors in SF such as Gardner Dozois and Terry Carr. We're also incredibly lucky to have the papers of contemporary writers such as Nalo Hopkinson, Jaymee Goh, Steven Barnes, Tananarive Due, and many, many more.

JPG: *What role do you think that academia plays in genre fiction?*

PA: Academic writing, like creative writing, like *all* writing, explores (and expresses) what it means to be human—and genre fiction has always been the literature of 'excess,' serving as a catch-all for subjects that fall outside of the realm of 'realism.'

(Personally, I believe that there is no such thing as 'realist' art—but that's a whole other conversation!)

I'm so grateful to work with the researchers, students, and faculty who use SF as a lens through which to think through our pasts, and present, and futures. It's oft-repeated that genre fiction has long lacked the 'respect' afforded other subjects in academia, but I've never really subscribed to narratives of respectability, and neither should anyone else. Do the thing, and find joy in it! Whether we call if SF or science fiction or speculative fiction or genre fiction or, or, or…

JPG: *What is the strangest item or artifact in the Eaton collection?*

PA: Strangest artifact? I have to name just one? Hmm, we have some pretty *interesting* items of memorabilia; I'd have to go with the Star Trek commemorative beer stein that's currently on display in our 'Unexpected Artifacts' exhibit. But that's just the tip of the iceberg!

JPG: *What is the rarest, or most precious, element of the collection?*

PA: Again, picking one is going to be hard, but I'd have to go with our copy of Margaret Cavendish's *The Blazing World* (1666) — which we've digitized, and made accessible in its entirety, online: The description of a new world, called the blazing world — Calisphere. https://calisphere.org/item/ark:/86086/n21v5hj5/

JPG: *What, in your opinion, is the importance of preservation, and what are the greatest challenges in today's archival processes?*

PA: We're very lucky to have a wonderful conservator, Christina Bean, here at UCR, who along with our processing archivist Andrew Lippert ensures that every item and every collection is properly stored. Christina also carries out repairs on any items that have been damaged, and builds custom mounts for objects we display in our exhibits.

In general, preservation is, of course, crucial within special collections—and one of the greatest challenges lies in archiving 'born digital' materials, such as emails and Word documents, whose formats may well become obsolete in ten/twenty/thirty years. The same is true of physical media formats such as VHS, DVD, etc. The process of stewarding these kinds of materials is ongoing and constantly evolving!

JPG: *Have the recent wave of book bans affected the Eaton, and what are the concerns of librarians in the recent rise of censorship and attacks on the free flow of information?*

PA: Thankfully, we haven't been affected by any book bans—most likely due to our location within a fairly liberal state (California). Every purchase I make for the Eaton has to be justified, and I take that responsibility very seriously; the items coming in must be of clear research value to the varied communities that we serve.

A popular maxim today is 'facts don't care about your feelings,' and that certainly goes for history, as it is reflected in archival collections. Literary history has always included—if not recognized or valued—work from marginalized creators: women, queer and trans authors, Black, Indigenous, disabled people, and people from the Global South. My job is to ensure that the Eaton Collection's holdings reflect, and celebrate, the full breadth of authors and artists working in speculative genres.

https://library.ucr.edu/collections/eaton-collection-of-science-fiction-fantasy

Photo by Stan Lim, UCR

Vinnie the Pacifist Virus
By Tara Campbell

DATE: Tuesday, Apr 18, 2124

FROM: Angela Mancinelli

TO: Nick Nickerson

Subject: Final Assignment: Vinnie the Pacifist Virus

Dear Prof. Nickerson,

Thanks for the extension on submitting my play for class. Turns out *both* twins wound up with the flu, which then spread to my older boy, then to my husband. I was taking care of the whole family. Whoo-boy, am I glad that's over!

I stayed up all night to get this in on time, so please excuse any typos.

Sincerely,
Angela Mancinelli

Attachment: Mancinelli_Vinnie_2_FINAL.docx

VINNIE THE PACIFIST VIRUS

A Play in One Act

by

Angela Mancinelli

Final Project for Drama 101
Nick Nickerson's Online School of
the Arts

Dramatis Personae

Vinnie: A virus from Jersey
Frankie: A virus from Jersey

Scene
Various members of the Mancinelli family.

Time
Every frickin' year, seems like.

<u>Scene 1</u>

SETTING: Throat, interior, concave "room" with rounded walls. Color of walls: muted pink with red splotches, liberally coated with mucous because someone didn't listen and just had to keep playing with those runny-nose kids down the street.

CURTAIN RISES on VINNIE, looking pensive. A few of the spindly hemagglutinin protruding all around his body are crossed like arms, and he's looking down. FRANKIE float-walks in stage left, looking self-satisfied.

VINNIE

Hey.

FRANKIE

Hey!

> (Gestures around at the inflamed throat)

Hell of a job, huh?

VINNIE

Yeah, hell of a job…

> (Looks briefly up and around at mucous and splotches on throat, then down again)

FRANKIE
(Looking closely at VINNIE)

Hey. Hey, what's eatin' you?

VINNIE

What? Nothin'.

FRANKIE

Nothin' my ass. You been down lately, like every day you're headin' to a funeral. What gives?

VINNIE

Funeral… Frankie, you ever… I dunno, you ever stop and think about what we're doin' here?

FRANKIE

What do you mean?

VINNIE

Well, I mean, all those cells just sittin' there, mindin' their own business…

FRANKIE

Yeah, well, that's how we like 'em, right? Nice and easy.

(Spots another couple of "marks" offstage, one stage left and one stage right. Nudges VINNIE.)

Which one you want?

VINNIE

You know, maybe I'll sit this one out…

FRANKIE

Come on, buddy. Come on, this is our thing, right? This is what we do!

VINNIE

(Deep sigh.)

Yeah, I guess it's what we do. I'll take the one over there.

(VINNIE hangs his head and float-walks stage left,
caving to peer pressure, like kids who keep sharing toys
with other germ-ridden little kids down the street, despite
being warned by their mother.)

FRANKIE

All right, see you on the flip side!

(Float-walks stage right, addressing cell offstage.)

Hey there, how you doin'? Mind if I dock up here?

(Big "pop" and splash of water from stage right.
FRANKIE strolls out, dusting off his ~~sleeves~~ ~~flagella~~
hemagglutinin [I guess I have to repeat this word since
viruses don't have arms or flagella — look up alternative
later].)

FRANKIE

Vinnie? You done?

(Big "pop" and splash of water from stage left. VINNIE
trudges out.)

There you are. What the hell took you so long?

VINNIE

(Shrugs)

Oh, you know, just lookin' around in there.

FRANKIE

What're you looking for in there? It's just a cell.

VINNIE

Well, yeah, but you know there's different kinds of cells.

FRANKIE

Yeah, so? What does it matter?

VINNIE

What, don't you wanna know anything about the world around you?

FRANKIE

What's to know? We're viruses. We get in there, multiply, and bust out; ba-da-boom, ba-da-bing, as they say. What else is there to know?

VINNIE

Jesus, Frankie, listen to you: "What's there to know?" You ain't curious? It don't matter to you where you're at?

FRANKIE

No it don't matter.

(Starts looking around for next "mark.")

Why should it matter? A cell's a cell.

(Points offstage left and right.)

And there's a couple of cells with our names on 'em, know what I'm sayin'?

VINNIE

All right, but do me a favor, just show a little respect, okay? Take a look around for a second and, I don't know, give thanks maybe before you start multiplyin'. All right?

FRANKIE

Yeah, yeah…

    (Exits stage left, speaking to object offstage)

Hey, how you doin'? Come here often?

    (VINNIE sighs and float-walks stage right.)

    (Big "pop" and splash of water from stage left.
    FRANKIE struts out like someone who thinks he's Mr.
    Big Shot 'cause he got his first kiss, way too young, if
    you ask me, 'cause being the oldest kid in the family
    doesn't mean someone's old enough to start dating, know
    what I mean, not to mention he probably spread the flu to
    his new "girlfriend")

FRANKIE

Vinnie! Vinnie! Aw, come on…

    (Big "pop" and splash of water from stage right. VINNIE
    enters and approaches FRANKIE expectantly.)

VINNIE

So, you notice anything?

FRANKIE

Yeah, sure it was nice...

VINNIE

You didn't even look, did you?

FRANKIE

I don't get it, what's there to look at?

(Starts searching for next pair of cells to go after, like kids who stay home sick from school stuffing their faces with chips all afternoon so they can't finish the dinner their mother slaved over all afternoon.)

VINNIE

Just take a look and tell me what it's like, all right? Is it cloudy or clear, what kinda things they got movin' around in there? Is it round, or long and skinny, or what? Okay?

FRANKIE

Yeah, okay.

VINNIE

Humor me.

FRANKIE

All right, all right already! Jeez! I'll be over in this one.

(Exits stage left, talking offstage.)

Hey, you look familiar. Haven't we met somewhere?

(VINNIE stalks off stage right. A few moments pass, then, simultaneously, loud "pops" and splashes from both stage left and stage right.)

FRANKIE

(Entering slowly.)

Huh.

                    VINNIE
        (Also entering slowly.)

See what I'm sayin'?

                    FRANKIE
        (Nodding.)

It was actually kinda nice in there, you know?

                    VINNIE
        (Also nodding.)

Yeah.

                    FRANKIE
Real quiet. Peaceful.

                    VINNIE
Uh-huh.

                    FRANKIE
All kinds of neat little squiggly things—

                    VINNIE
Mitochondria.

                    FRANKIE
Yeah, mitochondria floatin' around. Real delicate.

                    VINNIE
Yeah…

                    FRANKIE
And those cool, star-shaped tubey things—

VINNIE

Centrioles.

FRANKIE

Yeah. And that crazy wadded up thing—

VINNIE

Golgi apparatus.

FRANKIE
(Looks at VINNIE, impressed.)

Yeah. And that big ol' round nucleus in the middle'a all of it, just tryin' to keep it all together. Kind of a shame to go in and start bustin' everything up, you know? I wonder what…

> (His voice drifts off as he gets distracted by new cells floating around offstage.)

VINNIE

Uh-huh, I guess that's kinda what I was thinkin'. But, uh…

> (Notices FRANKIE looking around like an X-box addict too distracted to finish his frickin' homework without having to be yelled at for once.)

There's another couple of cells comin' our way.

FRANKIE

Yeah.

> (Hesitates.)

I guess we should go in.

VINNIE

Yeah, I guess we should.

FRANKIE

'Course, we already done a lot this week.

VINNIE

Yeah, we been busy.

FRANKIE

I mean, we prob'ly hit our quota already.

VINNIE

Oh yeah, we done hundreds, maybe thousands by now. I lost count.

FRANKIE

Me too. We don't wanna throw the numbers off, right? Set the bar too high?

VINNIE

Whooo, no, don't wanna get the other guys on our asses, huh?

FRANKIE

You got that right.

(Startled by what he sees offstage, stage right.)

Hey, what's that?

VINNIE

Aw shit. Antibodies.

FRANKIE

Crap, there goes the neighborhood.

(A great gust of wind blows in from stage left.)

VINNIE

Hey, did someone finally decide to try blowing their nose like
their mother asked, instead of wiping it on their sleeve? Maybe
we should hitch a ride; I think I'm ready for a change of scenery.

FRANKIE
(Cowering in wind, which then dies down a bit.)

I don't know, man; maybe we should just lay low for a while. I
don't wanna dry up in some Kleenex somewhere, seein' as how
someone will just leave it layin' on the floor 'cause they're
apparently too busy to throw it away like a civilized human.

VINNIE
(On guard for fluctuating wind currents)

Nah, you know what, I think this is gonna be a sneeze, and these
people never cover their mouths when they sneeze, no matter
how many times their beleaguered mother asks them to. Plus,
they'll never reach a Kleenex soon enough, so we'll be nice and
mobile, with access to everything they touch. It's now or never,
man. Ready?

FRANKIE
Yeah, all right. Wait for it…

(Wind gusts again, accompanied by a massive sneezing
sound.)

VINNIE
Okay, let's go!

(Bright white lights flood the stage and out into the

audience. FRANKIE AND VINNIE jump and are blown
off stage right.)

(BLACKOUT)

(END OF SCENE)

<u>Scene 2</u>

SETTING: Grimy white poodle fluff, because it would apparently kill the kids to bathe her once in a while.

CURTAIN RISES on VINNIE and FRANKIE stumbling to their feet.

VINNIE

Frankie, you still there?

FRANKIE

Yeah, yeah, I'm right here. But where the hell are we?

VINNIE

Oh god, what is this?

FRANKIE

Aw crap, Vinnie. This is fur!

VINNIE

Aw fer chrissake! I knew that damn poodle was nothin' but trouble.

FRANKIE

Aw geez, Vinnie, we can't do our thing here. We ain't compatible. We gotta find a way outta here or it's all over for us.

VINNIE
(Standing tall with dignity.)

Frankie, it's been an honor workin' wit' you.

FRANKIE

What the hell, Vinnie, you can't just give up. Do somethin'! You know, I heard about these guys who survived on fleas for a week before they hitched a hand to another human. Come on, start lookin'!

VINNIE

Fleas, Frankie? Let's go out wit' a little grace.

In a way, I kinda don't mind, you know? I mean, we're kinda like heroes.

FRANKIE

What the hell are you talkin' about?

VINNIE

Well, the way I see it, we don't gotta ruin any more cells, you know? We can just sit back and enjoy a peaceful end, not hurtin' nobody else.

FRANKIE

So what, we just give up?

(Puts hand to chest. Bends hemagglutinin toward main structure. [fix later])

Ooff, I don't feel so good.

VINNIE

Ah come on, it's all in your head [Mind? Central viral processing center? More research needed here]. We got hours yet. You're just thinkin' about it too much.

FRANKIE

So what else am I supposed to do, just sit here and wait?

                            VINNIE
I don’t know.

        (pauses, twiddling hemagglutinin)

You bring any games?

                            FRANKIE
No I didn’t bring any frickin’ games. What am I, your mother?

                            VINNIE
I don’t know.

        (Nudges FRANKIE.)

You could be.

                            FRANKIE
Asshole.

        (Shakes head.)

Yeah, I guess I could be.

Ain’t that a thing, how that all works. We’re all so busy just
multiplyin’ and multiplyin’, I don’t know who’s who anymore. I
mean, I don’t think I could pick my own kids out of a lineup.

                            VINNIE
I know, man. I mean, who do you know, besides me? I mean,
really know?

                            FRANKIE
        (Taking offense.)

What, you're so popular? Who do YOU know Mr. Big Shot?

VINNIE

Nobody! That's my point! Look at us, man, just runnin' around, makin' more of ourselves, but who do we really know?

(Pauses.)

All I'm sayin' is maybe this is an opportunity. Look, we can't infect this dog. Maybe we can take the opportunity to just, you know, get to know some organisms around here.

FRANKIE
(Putting hand to head, grimacing slightly.)

What, you mean, not hijack 'em? Just — talk to 'em?

VINNIE

Yeah. Maybe.

(Folds slightly in on self, as if he has a cramp.)

How about it? We'll change history!

FRANKIE
(Scoffs.)

Yeah, Vinnie the Pacifist Virus. Where's your frickin' medal?

(Increasingly weak.)

I don't know, Vinnie, I don't feel so good at all.

                    VINNIE

Me neither.

          (Groans and clutches self harder.)

Man, I didn't think we'd go out this quick.

          (Both viruses exhibit signs of suffering.)

                    FRANKIE

Aw shit, man, I don't wanna die.

                    VINNIE
          (Grunting.)

Who does, man? But we'll go out heroes.

                    FRANKIE

Heroes? Who's gonna even know?

                    VINNIE
          (The thought shocks him so much he stops writhing in
          pain for a moment.)

                    FRANKIE

Yeah, genius. I don't see no paparazzi around, do you? We die
like "heroes" out here, who the hell's gonna know?

                    VINNIE
          (Bowls over with a new spasm of pain.)

Aw crap. Where's those frickin' fleas?

(The lights start to dim. VINNIE and FRANKIE look up.)

FRANKIE

What the hell is that?

(They look around, as the lights grow dimmer and dimmer.)

VINNIE

(Gasps, excited.)

Holy shit, I think this is our helping hand — like, literally. On the count of three, jump, okay? You with me?

(FRANKIE nods frantically.)

Okay: One…

(The lights grow dimmer…)

Two…

(And dimmer…)

Three!

(FRANKIE and VINNIE jump.)

(BLACKOUT)

(END OF SCENE)

Scene 3

SETTING: Throat, interior, concave "room" with rounded, pink, healthy walls despite never washing her hands like her mother asks her to. But just wait…

CURTAIN RISES on VINNIE and FRANKIE stumbling to their ~~feet~~ [ah crap, stumbling upright, whatever that is for a virus, fix later].

VINNIE

(Looking around.)

You see this, Frankie?

FRANKIE

(Shell-shocked but relieved.)

Holy shit, are we where I think we are?

VINNIE

Frankie, we made it! I think it's the sister!

(High-fives FRANKIE and looks up.)

Bless you, little girl, for never washing your hands!

FRANKIE

(Starting to warm up to the idea of not being doomed.)

She ain't been sick yet this year, has she?

VINNIE

Nope, no antibodies here.

(Energized.)

Frankie, we made it! This is a sign! This is our chance to really make a difference.

(Looks offstage.)

And I see a couple of fine-lookin' cells at two o'clock…

FRANKIE

Whoa, whoa, whoa, hold on. What happened to the whole peacenik-pacifist thing?

VINNIE

No, man, you don't get it. I'm a new virus now. I meant what I said; I'm gonna make new friends, learn new things. I hear there's alternatives to asexual reproduction.

(Nudges FRANKIE.)

FRANKIE

Come on, Vinnie. A virus is a virus.

VINNIE

We can mutate.

FRANKIE

You can maybe. I can't.

VINNIE

Frankie, just give it a try. Just once. Come on, I got you a hitch on that hand, I saved your life.

FRANKIE

I don't know man.

                              VINNIE
Come on, give it a shot! Just follow my lead.

                             FRANKIE
        (Shaking his head.)

I know how this is gonna end…

                              VINNIE
        (Gives FRANKIE a warning look.)

Well, for once don't follow your instinct. Just let me do the
talkin'.

        (To cells offstage, stage left.)

Hey there, we're new to town. You got a minute?

        (FRANKIE AND VINNIE exit stage left.)

        (Wait ten seconds.)

(If someone in the
audience coughs
within those ten
seconds cause they
didn't take a cough
drop before the play
like a decent
person: two loud
"pops" and splashes
of water from stage
left.)

(BLACKOUT)

(END OF SCENE)

(END OF PLAY)

(BUT, if nobody coughs in ten seconds: FRANKIE AND VINNIE stroll back onto stage from stage left, looking self-satisfied.)

FRANKIE

I gotta hand it to you, Vinnie. That wasn't half bad.

VINNIE

The locals are certainly friendly, aren't they?

(They laugh and pat each other with their spindly hemagglutinin on what would be their backs.)

So, uh… You gonna call yours tomorrow?

FRANKIE

What, are we supposed to?

VINNIE

I don't know. I kinda got the feeling from mine—

FRANKIE

Yeah, mine kinda said something about that too.

VINNIE

Who knew about this part, right?

FRANKIE

Yeah, I know. Especially with all these other new cells around.

(Nodding offstage)

Hey, how you doin'?

VINNIE

Yeah, I know, right? But… So you gonna call tomorrow?

FRANKIE

Maybe, I dunno… I guess so… Yeah.

VINNIE

Yeah, me too.

FRANKIE

So… Do we get to meet new cells, like, before tomorrow?

VINNIE

I dunno, I ain't so sure about that.

FRANKIE

Jeez, this mutation crap is complicated. It better be worth it.

VINNIE

(Looking around optimistically, enjoying the sights.
Meanwhile, bubbles pour in from both sides, and offstage
female voices coo things like "Ooh, there they are," and
"Are those are the new guys?" and "I hear they got a
new--technique.")
You know, Frankie…

(Looping a couple of hemagglutinin around where
FRANKIE's shoulders would be, if he had any.)

Somethin' tells me it will be.

(BLACKOUT)

(END OF SCENE)

(END OF PLAY)

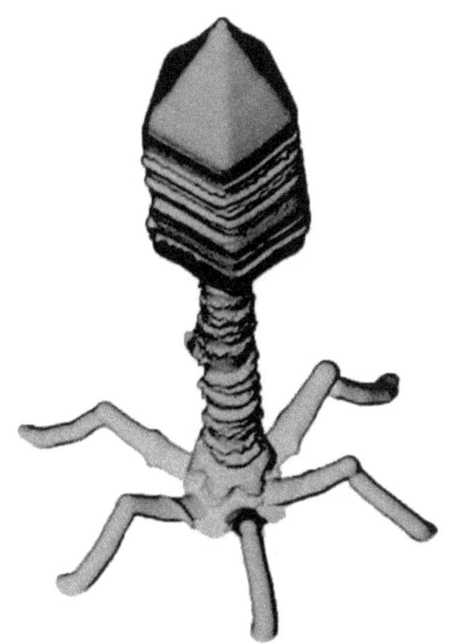

Contributor Bios:

Phoenix Alexander (he/him) is a queer, Greek-Cypriot author and curator of SF/F and horror. He is the Editor-in-Chief of *Vector: the Journal of the British Science Fiction Association*, and has published over 30 short stories and articles. He holds a Ph.D. in English and African American Studies from Yale University, and a BA and MA from Queen Mary, University of London. In his day job, he is the curator of the Eaton Collection of Science Fiction and Fantasy at the University of California, Riverside, where he stewards one of the world's largest cataloged collections of science fiction, fantasy, and other genre materials.

Eugen Bacon is an African Australian author. She is a Solstice, British Fantasy, Ignyte, Locus and Foreword Indies Award winner. She's also a twice World Fantasy and Shirley Jackson Award finalist, and a finalist in the Philip K. Dick Awards and the Nommo Awards for speculative fiction by Africans. Eugen is an Otherwise Fellow, and was announced on the honor list for 'doing exciting work in gender and speculative fiction'. *Danged Black Thing* made the Otherwise Award Honor List as a 'sharp collection of Afro-Surrealist work'. Visit her at eugenbacon.com.

Michael Butterworth is a UK author, publisher and editor. He was a key figure among the younger writers of the UK New Wave of Science Fiction in the 1960's, contributing fiction to *New Worlds* throughout the magazine's existence. This led to him in 1975 co-founding Savoy Books with David Britton and co-authoring Britton's controversial novel *Lord Horror*. In 2009 he launched the contemporary visual art and writing journal, *Corridor8*. He is the author of twenty books, the most recent being *Michael Butterworth: Complete Poems 1965-2020* (Space Cowboy Books, 2023), a collection of his 'New Wave' writing *Butterworth* (NULL23, 2019), a novel *My Servant the Wind* (also NULL23 2019) and his memoir *The Blue Monday Diaries: In the*

Studio with New Order (Plexus Books, 2016). He is at work on two further memoirs, *The Sunshine Island* about his father who had OCD, *Driven by Anger* about his mother and a novel, *Withersoever.*

Tara Campbell is a writer, teacher, Kimbilio Fellow, and fiction co-editor at Barrelhouse. Publication credits include *Masters Review, Wigleaf, Electric Literature, CRAFT Literary, Uncharted Magazine, Daily Science Fiction, Strange Horizons,* and *Escape Pod/Artemis Rising.* She's the author of the eco sci-fi novel *TreeVolution,* two hybrid collections of poetry and prose, and two short story collections. Her sixth book, City of Dancing Gargoyles (SFWP), was a finalist for the 2025 Philip K. Dick Award. She's taught creative writing at venues such as Johns Hopkins University, American University, Clarion West, The Writer's Center, and Hugo House. Find her at www.taracampbell.com

John Clute has been writing SF and fantasy criticism since the 1960s, much of which has been assembled in several collections, beginning with *Strokes* (1988); he has been involved in writing encyclopedias since the 1970s. His novel *Appleseed* (2001) was a *New York Times* Notable Book in 2002. He is currently working on the fourth edition (online from 2021) of *The Encyclopedia of Science Fiction* and its affiliated Substack.

Gregory Feeley writes science fiction, fantasy, historical, and contemporary fiction. His most recent publication is a chapbook, *Cumberworld & Farther: Three Stories.*

The editor was unable to find any biographical information concerning **Alice W. Fuller** except an obituary which could not be confirmed as being for the same person. If you have any information please get in touch.

Jean-Paul L. Garnier is the owner of Space Cowboy Books bookstore and publishing house, producer of *Simultaneous Times Podcast* (2023 & 25 Laureate Award Winner, 2024 BSFA, Ignyte, and British Fantasy Award Finalist), and was the editor of the SFPA's *Star*Line* magazine from 2021-2025. He is currently the poetry editor of *Worlds of IF* & *Galaxy* magazines. In 2024 he won the Laureate Award for Best Editor. He has written many books of poetry and science fiction.

Rocco Harris, also known, in some uncertain circles, as doctor auxiliary or fall precauxions—is a composer, performer and producer of music, often of a moody and introspective nature. His works have accompanied modern dance, science fiction podcasts, and other interdisciplinary works.
Recordings of his most recent efforts can be found here: doctorauxiliary.bandcamp.com
Recordings of some of his works for acoustic ensembles can be found here: soundcloud.com/roccoharris78
Rocco can be reached in all the obvious online haunts for conversation & potential collaboration

James Machell is a British writer, born in London and matured in Seoul. He is a contributor to the *Encyclopedia of Science Fiction* and the outreach manager for *Utopia Science Fiction Magazine* for which he gets to interview his favourite writers and artists, including P. Djèlí Clark, Ken Liu, and Samuel R Delany. He is also the contest chair for the Science Fiction & Fantasy Poetry Association and a judge for The Latin Programme Poetry Prize.

Charles Platt used to write science fiction but was subsequently one of three senior writers at *Wired* magazine during its halcyon years. Now he writes books about electronics and builds rapid cooling equipment for a cryonics organization.

Other Titles from
Space Cowboy Books

Books:

Space Exploration: Strange New Worlds – John C. Mannone

One Way & Other Stories – Miriam Allen deFord

Life During the Lazarus Age – Robert Frazier

Dreaming of Autonomous Vehicles – Jaroslav Olša, Jr.

The Future is Brief – Jean-Paul L. Garnier

Wave IX – Various Authors

The Martians – Emilie Procházková

Mexicans on the Moon – Pedro Iniguez

Another Time: Time Travel Stories 1942–1960

Complete Poems 1965–2020 – Michael Butterworth

Simultaneous Times Vol. 3 – Various Authors

Simultaneous Times Vol. 2.5 – Various Authors

Simultaneous Times Vol. 2 – Various Authors

Simultaneous Times Vol. 1 – Various Authors

Garbage In, Gospel Out – Jean-Paul L. Garnier

Betelgeuse Dimming – Jean-Paul L. Garnier

Future Anthropology – Jean-Paul L. Garnier

Chapbooks:

The Reducing Flame – Richard Magahiz

Micropoetry for Microplanets – Brian U. Garrison

Shelf Life – F. J. Bergmann

Mars Maundering – Denise Dumars

www.spacecowboybooks.com

SPACE
COWBOY